INSIDER

JILLIAN JACOBS

GREEN MOOSE PRODUCTIONS

JILLIANJACOBS.COM

The Infidelity Corporation will broker relationships—for a price. Their clients are exclusive and successful, their employees confidential and classified. Infidelity ensures that CEOs, politicians, and high-profile artists find love, with their friends and relatives none the wiser about how the happy couple met. But twists and turns abound in a world where old money, new money, and no money clash, from West Coast to East Coast and beyond. Enter Infidelity's world of entrapment, betrayal, and deceit, where you decide whose relationship is real and whose is just an agreement.

INSIDER

Infidelity insider Imina Lesedi is forbidden to share her employer's secrets—and her own. Only one man understands the delicate nature of working for a company that provides companionship for the elite, but his social and financial status make him unattainable, even though Imina craves a visit to his darkroom.

Award winning photographer Aiden Maxfield views life from behind the camera. A charmer by nature, he relishes the moments he makes the elusive Imina smile—but he would much rather picture the exotic beauty on his rumpled sheets.

When the two are trapped together, the enticement proves too strong to resist. Raw passions are exposed, and their years of denial culminate in an insatiable desire for more.

But not everyone celebrates their newfound bliss. A malicious foe is threatened by Imina's knowledge of a dark secret from their shared past. When that truth is exposed, Imina and Aiden must fight for their love before it becomes shuttered by lies, deception—and Infidelity.

To Readers:
Because of you, I get to escape into different worlds for a time.
Thank you.

ACKNOWLEDGMENTS

Greatest appreciation to Aleatha Romig for being an author advocate.

CHAPTER ONE

Whistling along with the instrumental playing through the overhead speakers, Aiden Maxfield gently placed his camera into its hard plastic case before laying it in his bag.

Today's photo shoot had gone well. The woman, Alexandria, held her chin high, yet he sensed a slight undercurrent of anxiety. Her conflicting emotions were completely understandable. After all, something had led the woman to Infidelity's doors.

The woman would soon be paired with an obscenely wealthy Infidelity client. *Infidelity*. Aiden shook his head over the word. He'd never understood the company's name. A company that assigned two people to a year-long contract should be titled Fidelity. Although, the possibility existed that some clients *were* married, he couldn't say, as he'd never met them. However, the company's purpose was companionship. If that hadn't been the case, he wouldn't have agreed to work here.

Speaking of companionship, he wondered if today would be the day Ms. Imina Lesedi would agree to a drink after work. He'd only been able to wave a brief hello, before heading back to set up the photo shoot.

As he stepped into the hallway, he slung his camera bag over his shoulder and hummed along to the tune still playing overhead. Setting his bag against Imina's desk, Aiden flicked a glance at the tawny-skinned beauty. Each time he saw her, his behavior reverted to that of a grade-school boy at recess. He mentally shrugged. So what if he delighted in seeing the flare in her deep brown eyes? Placing his hand over this heart, he sang the words to the song. "And we rocked all night long."

Imina rubbed a hand over her mouth, covering the slight upward curve of her lips. "What are you doing?"

"Serenading you." He bopped his head back and forth and belted out the lyrics, keeping his eye on Ms. I'm-Pretending-You-Don't-Exist the entire time. "Yeah, yeah, all night...we rocked it, yeah, we rocked it." He'd just begun his air-guitar solo when Imina bolted out of her office chair.

"That's enough for today." Rolling her eyes, she grabbed her cell phone off the desk. "Time for you to go."

"As you wish." Holding back a grin, Aiden swept a hand before him. "Lead the way."

In her black leather shoes, likely designer, Imina rounded her art-deco desk and stepped toward the elevator.

As always, when walking through Infidelity's front lobby, he considered again what led clients here? Located within a blue glass building with a distinctive curved façade in downtown New York City, Infidelity serviced lonely hearts out of the top two floors. Imina greeted each candidate before they met with Karen Flores, the intake representative.

Imina was never any help with his contemplations. She'd never revealed anyone's secrets, including her own. Sure, he could get her to talk weather, politics, current Broadway shows, but anytime he tried to go deeper, asking about her family or her love life—even a possible love life with him, she clammed up. Her icy attitude hadn't stopped him from asking though.

He admired her fidelity even when it drove him crazy. Her

professionalism. Her protective stance for her employer, Karen. Her quick wit. Her beauty. All added up to an incredible woman.

Over the last three years, he'd learned what made her smile, laugh, frown, but he'd come to crave something more. Imina wasn't indifferent to his presence, or she wouldn't rant and rage—eyes lit and tongue sharp. Still, no matter how often he asked, he couldn't even get her to agree to a cup of coffee.

Yet, even with her continual denials, he'd follow her petite body, currently swishing across the gray carpet in a black skirt and white button-down top, anywhere. He imagined sliding up behind her and caressing each soft curve, but he appreciated having all his teeth.

Not happening, Maxfield.

Sighing, he followed, checking the time on his phone. An hour of travel remained before his next appointment. In a city like New York, he never knew what might hold up a cab, so he always left a buffer between appointments. Right now, he had a little more time to dig under Ms. Lesedi's skin—one of his favorite past times. "Let me guess, the lady who just left...Alexandria, right? She's from where? Mississippi? Her Southern accent was barely discernible but still there. Everything about her screamed money, so why was she joining the Infidelity line-up?"

"After three years of questions about our new employees, why would you believe I'd answer now?" Arching a perfectly-sculpted brow, Imina glanced over her shoulder. "You know I can't talk about them. At all."

Alexandria Collins, looked completely different from the caramel-skinned, brown-eyed, dark-haired spitfire standing before him with both arms crossed against her chest. Imina's typical stance when facing him. He chuckled again. "When do you ever want to talk about anything?"

"Exactly." She flashed a fake smile—tongue firmly in cheek.

Tucking his phone in his leather satchel, Aiden followed his nemesis to the private elevator.

Once inside, she hit the button for the 37th floor.

Aiden stepped in behind her and remained at her side, even though they were alone. A special passkey was necessary to get to Imina's floor, but he didn't need anything special to stand next to her. "Go ahead and take me to the lobby. I have another shoot across town." He adjusted the shoulder strap on his bag.

"You can go down from thirty-seven on your own." Imina leaned against the elevator's brass railing. "I don't have time to hold your hand."

"Ah, but I want you to." He grinned.

She rolled her eyes. "Ply your wares elsewhere."

"One day I'll stop asking, and you'll wish you'd said yes."

"Doubtful." She bit her lower lip and shook her head. "I think you should—"

The elevator lights blinked off and on.

Their downward motion slowed then lurched to a hard stop.

Imina wobbled on her heels, stumbling forward.

"What the...." Aiden caught her before she fell, holding her against him. "What happened?" He breathed in the scent of vanilla with a hint of cinnamon from the gum she always had on her desk.

Imina stiffened. "Are we going to drop?"

"We won't drop."

"How can you know?" She turned in his arms, eyes wide. "We could fall to our deaths."

"Give it a second. The elevator will power back on."

"I just had maintenance on this a month ago." She frowned at the panel before pressing a few buttons. "What do you think happened?"

"Imina." Aiden clutched her face between his hands. "It's okay. During New York's World Fair back in like...I think 1854, Elisha Otis created the "safety" elevator which is why elevator occupants no longer fall to their doom."

"I don't have time for your history lessons. Save them for your picture books." Imina flicked a strand of slightly wavy hair over her shoulder. "I'm calling Karen." She punched in numbers on her cell phone. "Come on, come on. Hello...Karen, the elevator's stuck. Can you contact maintenance?...What?...Oh, they know...well, what are they doing?...That's insane...what's their number?...No, it isn't dark in here...the cameras aren't working, either?...Fine...Aiden's with me." She cleared her throat, and then her cheeks turned a little pink. "No, Karen...I've told you why...He's standing right here, so call back when you know more." Disconnecting from the call, Imina huffed out a sigh. "Karen says maintenance is aware of the issue, and they should have things up and going in about an hour." She jabbed all the panel buttons with her manicured finger. "She says the camera's out. All they see is a blank screen." Imina pressed and held her finger against the red Emergency Call button. "We'll probably plummet to our deaths."

"I explained why we won't die. Now stop." Aiden pulled her hand from the panel. "You'll poke a hole in that thing. Quit pushing the buttons."

"I don't understand why the back-up generators aren't kicking on. This makes no sense."

"Imina, nothing we can do." Aiden shoved both hands in his jeans pockets. "Just relax."

"Don't tell me to relax." Imina poked a finger against his chest. "Karen is up in her office all alone. Part of my job is security. I'm the front line."

"First off, quit trying to injure objects with your finger." Aiden grabbed her hand and pressed it against his chest. "No one can access her."

"If someone wanted to, they could." Imina yanked her hand free then ran her fingers through her hair.

Aiden furrowed his brow. Infidelity had extreme security measures in place. No one could even access the offices without a keycard, so why was she so concerned? He did know Imina took a boxing class. Maybe she even carried a gun. And why was the vision of her wearing nothing but a gun holster so hot? He blinked and shook his head. "Why are you worried? Unhappy clients?"

"Shhh..." Imina placed a finger against her mauve-colored lips. "We are not discussing Infidelity in this elevator."

"You started it." Aiden grinned. His Imina was a paranoid one, probably because she'd ordered the surveillance and knew who was listening. "If I were a client, I'd pick you."

Her eyes widened. "I'm *not* an employee. Well, I am but not in that way."

"You could be."

"No." She averted her gaze then punched the Intercom button, which did nothing.

Interesting. Why was she so against being on the client list? "Since we're stuck here, why don't you tell me how you came to work for Infidelity?"

"No." She'd given up on the panel and had her fingers locked on the edge of the elevator doors. Trying to wrench them open, she grunted and her sculpted arms tightened as she tugged.

"All right." He wrapped an arm around her waist and dragged her away. "Stop. You're fidgeting."

"Remove your hands from my person."

"Oh, the haughty-voice. I love that one." He leaned down and breathed in her sweet vanilla scent. "I think about that voice sometimes when I'm—"

She shoved away. "Shut it, Maxfield. I'm not one of your fawning women."

Leaning against the elevator wall, he crossed one ankle over the other, noting a black scuff on his brown dress shoes. He wasn't overly particular about his appearance. Like today, jeans and a button-up shirt were generally all he needed. "I'm not dressed to impress. I don't know why you think I have fawning women?" He studied her for a moment. Now was a good time to clear the air between them. Maybe he could discover why she was so adamant about denying what they could be together. "As usual, you're making assumptions that are completely unfounded."

"I don't make assumptions." She smoothed down her skirt. "I

know everything about each person who walks through Infidelity's door."

He shrugged. "You know what's on the surface."

"I don't need to know the rest."

"Why not?"

Imina glared. "Listen. *Again.* If I need a man, I'll find one. You want to talk about Infidelity? Why it works? Because money makes things easier. People seek companionship because they're tired of fitting into labels. Mother, daughter, sister, assistant...whatever. All those definitions mask who we are at our core. Infidelity creates a relationship with set parameters. No guessing games. No stressing over where the relationship is going. Everything is chosen for the client *and* the employee."

"Why would anyone *want* to know?" Frowning, Aiden flicked his wrist in the air. "That's the beauty of falling in love. The anguish, the pain, the passion. Love isn't easy. Shouldn't be...if it's real."

"Too much in life is hard." Imina sniffed. "And love is never real."

Ah, now they were getting somewhere. The only people who didn't believe in love were those who'd been hurt by it. Who'd hurt her? Instead of delving into that topic, he tossed out a dare. "If all you need is a man, I'm right here. I have been for years. No need to look any further."

"Too messy." She pressed the down button again.

"Yeah, it will be." Aiden straightened, reached out and pulled her hand from the panel then wrapped it around his waist. Inches from her luscious mouth, he halted, licking his lips.

Her breath hitched.

He angled his head and—

Her phone rang.

She gazed at his mouth for a moment before turning away and answering the call. "Karen...still an hour? Fine...yes, we're okay... Thank you." After she hung up, she met his gaze. "An hour."

"Well then, shall we continue?" He tucked her hair behind her ear.

She leaned into his touch then, eyes-wide, she stumbled back a step and sighed. "You say I don't know you, but I know the company you keep."

"The company I keep?" Aiden furrowed his brow. "What's that mean?"

"Forget I said anything." Imina fiddled with the top button of her blouse. "It was a mistake."

OH, Lord, she'd almost slipped.

Aiden Maxfield, a man who would know about money and class, leaned against the elevator railing in his usual slouchy, I'm-too-sexy-to-live stance. In his designer jeans and button-down teal shirt, he tilted his head and gave a half-smile. "I've got you hostage in this elevator, so let's get down to some real truths."

"About what?" She'd love to get real with him. Something about his cocky smile always ratcheted up her libido. Plus, his dark hair, soulful brown eyes, sharp cheekbones, and full lips—the man would look amazing lying across her bed—or across the elevator floor. Hmmm...with an hour, that thought had some merit.

"Let's start with your comment about the company I keep. What did you mean?"

"All right. Fine." Imina did enjoy their little chats, not that she'd ever admit that to him. They were friends, of a sort. She could actually talk to him about where she worked. Every time he stopped by her desk, she inwardly cursed when her traitorous heart stuttered a little. Didn't matter. A Maxfield had no business being with a nobody from Cape Town, South Africa, of Cape Coloured descent. She hated having those thoughts, but she did. "Aiden, where would you ever see us going? Your family and the company you keep is the *old* money crowd. The Upper-East-side crowd. The never-look-at-the-menu-prices crowd. Plus all your stylist friends, actors, actresses, and models. You like being in the spotlight, and I don't. We might have a few hot nights in the bedroom, but I think you're looking for more… and that's not on the table."

"Why not?"

Imina stared up at the ceiling, shaking her head. *Why not?* Hadn't she fantasized about intimate moments with him? She worked for a company that provided companionship, and the one man she could see becoming that for her, was the one man she couldn't have. But maybe? Just once? Just today. "Here's why not, Mr. Always-So-Nosy. Traumatic sexual experiences have ruined my belief in a happily ever after. My psychologist says I have a borderline personality disorder, which means I have trouble controlling my impulses and regulating my emotions. I do crazy things for crazy reasons. Sex, alcohol, the occasional drug use. She says I sabotage myself because I don't have enough self-worth. I think she's wrong. So I'm a little wild sometimes. I'm young and not hurting anyone so who cares?" She shrugged. "And, just to be clear, I only see her because Karen makes me go. I know who I am, and why I am. It is what it is."

"I know who you are, too. And I'd love to be wild with you. Calm, too. We could do both. So, why not give us a go?"

Imina tucked her tongue in her cheek. Why did he always have to push? Always pecking away until she wanted to scream. Fine…she would scream—in a more pleasurable way. Why not go wild? Explore? Plus, this conversation revealed way too much, and if it continued, he might discover truths that had to stay hidden. He wanted to give them a go? They would. Right here. Right now. That'd be one sure way to shut down his inquisitive mind. "Listen, we can continue to dig into my mental health history, or we can pursue a conversation that's a little more…intimate." Imina unbuttoned the top two buttons of her shirt, revealing her black lace bra. "I'm willing to pass the time without any more talking. What do you say?" She arched a brow.

Aiden studied her for a moment. "I'm sorry, what?" His gaze dropped to her open blouse before he lifted a finger and ran it down her collarbone.

Fighting back a shiver, she dropped to her knees, giving in to a craving she'd had for years. Tugging on his zipper, she gazed up at him and repeated his question from earlier. "Shall we continue?"

He cupped her cheek in his hand. "Why now?"

"I'm on my knees, and you're asking why now?" She frowned, very sure she didn't want to answer his question or reflect on the monumental mistake this could be. With the heady scent of his arousal filling her senses, she only wanted to focus on pleasure. On taste. On touch. "I believe you said you wanted to be wild with me... well..." Licking her lips, she ran a hand up his thigh. "Why now? Why *not* now? We're trapped in an elevator. Elevator sex is hot, and it's something we both want. You can't tell me you're not into the dirty and dangerous, because I know better."

"You know because of the *supposed* company I keep, right?"

Damn it! He had to let that go. She had to make him forget she'd ever made that slip. "Absolutely. All those naughty friends of yours... just think, now you'll have your own sordid tale to tell."

"Maybe I already have some." Aiden brushed her hair over her shoulder.

"Well." She licked her lips again. "Let's add another." Pulse thrumming, she widened the placket on his jeans and ran her nose along the thick, hard length of him, breathing in the essence of musk and man. "Mmm...you smell so good." She reveled in the power of holding a man's cock in her hand. *She* was in control. *She* could give or take pleasure.

As a teen, and for a very short time five years ago, she'd been on the receiving end of unpleasant, even painful experiences, but never again.

An hour with Aiden Maxfield she could do, but no more. She'd dreamed of him, ached even, but one of his best friends was her worst nightmare, so she'd steered clear...until now.

She freed his rigid cock from the confines of his boxer briefs and licked the mushroomed head before burying her nose in his trimmed dark brown hairs. Fuck, she loved sex. Loved the smell. The sweat.

The pleasure. She'd bend over right now and let Aiden fuck her into the railing, but they didn't have time, and she could only have a small taste. Gently caressing his sac with one hand, she locked her other hand around the root of his erection and worked him in and out of her mouth.

"Oh, hell yes, Imina. Take it all," Aiden hissed.

She swirled her tongue along his tip, and then traced a long vein down his length before engulfing him again. Pre-cum covered her tongue, and she greedily swallowed each drop.

With a groan, he gripped her hair and rocked gently into her mouth.

She slipped her middle finger in her mouth, alongside his cock, wetting it.

Increasing her suction, she slid her wet finger across his velvety sac and along the crease of his backside. Easing away, she smiled up at him. "Spread your legs. This is about to get much better."

Cheeks flushed, he caressed her bottom lip with his thumb. "Whatever you want, Imina."

His husky tone had her insides twisting, and she wished his fingers were buried deep within her pulsing, wet core. Tugging down his jeans to his ankles, she winked before brushing her wet middle finger across his puckered hole. "Do you want me to touch you here?"

"Yes. Do it."

Biting her bottom lip, she eased past the tight ring of muscle then worked in and out of his taut hole, pinging his prostate. That'd send a zing straight to his cock.

As expected, his legs wobbled, and his grip tightened in her hair. "Oh, fuck. That's the spot."

She smiled against his cock and pulled out her finger until just the tip remained before slamming back in again. She nipped the edge of his dripping cock then licked the head and slid him down her throat. Over and over, his hot cock hit the back of her throat as she pinged his hidden gland with her finger.

His harsh breath and mumbled curses had her on the edge of

coming herself. Shivers traveled down her spine to her core. Dirty, hot, edgy, sex with him wouldn't have any rules. She wasn't a sweet innocent, and now he'd know she was skilled in all the ways to please a man.

Suddenly, his ass tightened its grip on her finger, and he cursed. "I'm coming, and I want you to take it all. Don't stop."

His commanding tone shot straight to her core. Fuck! A dominant Aiden was sexy as hell. Because of that, she willingly accepted his command, sliding her finger in and out of his stretched hole faster and faster while working his erection with her other hand and her mouth, drawing in her cheeks with each pull.

Fingers tightening in her hair, he jerked just before his cock poured hot streams down her throat.

Humming against his dick, she closed her eyes, took his pleasure, and prayed that after today she wouldn't crave him even more. His cries of ecstasy seemed multiplied in the small space. Oh, what she could do with his body on her bed—tied and bound. The vision of Aiden at her mercy shot heat through her, making her moan. Swallowing the last drop, she leaned against his thigh and smiled. Finally. They only had this hour, and she'd take it. After three years of wanting a taste of this man, now she knew. Oh, fuck, how she knew.

With a groan, Aiden eased his flaccid cock from her mouth, and she slowly removed her finger from deep within his body.

He dropped to his knees and gripped her face between both hands. "Imina, let me take you home. Let me give you pleasure, too. Let me take my time without fear of discovery."

Fear? He knew nothing of her fear. Deep fear. Unending fear. But, as he covered her lips with his, driving deep with his tongue, she absolutely wished she felt otherwise.

CHAPTER TWO

Kellogg Brown straightened his tie in the cracked mirror. He'd been gone from the office longer than usual, but he'd cleared his schedule this afternoon, because he'd needed time to get across town to a neighborhood someone like him had no business visiting. Needed time to sate his unique desires.

He spared a glance at the whimpering woman sitting on the rumpled sheets of the hotel bed. Dim lighting, the stale cigarette scent imbedded into the yellow walls, and the heroin needle on the side table all added to the seedy atmosphere. He hated it and loved it. Craved it and despised it. "Enough with the crying. I paid you well, so shut up."

Gritting his teeth, he pulled his gaze away from the man in the mirror. He'd done it again. This time, he'd gone without for two full months. He hated the filthy room. The whores with the track marks up and down their arms. Hated to need anything this much.

He had a beautiful wife. Two kids. But, just like the woman behind him, he needed his fix. His father had paraded his women in front of his mother, not something Kellogg would ever do. He wasn't that crass.

Work pressure. Money pressure. Due to his high-stakes job at Demetri Enterprises, everything came to a head, and he needed release. Real release. And didn't he deserve it? He certainly paid these bitches well, probably more than they'd see from the average John. So why not throw in a couple more bills to get what he really wanted? Control. Domination. Both edged with pain. His pain. Her pain. He didn't care. He wanted to fuck with abandon. Over and over until he was covered in sweat and cum. Until the woman beneath him cried, screamed, and fought. He liked the scrappy ones, and today's treat had been a handful. He smiled as he took in the long, red scratches on his arm. Yes, today had gone very well.

Years ago, he'd made the mistake of signing a contract for what was essentially a high-end hookup, but the whole thing had ended in disaster. Never again. Now he came to the shit end of town. Used a shit hotel and kicked each stupid, crying cunt from the room once he'd finished. "I warned you, but you said you needed the cash. Take a shower and get out." Fury boiled in his chest. He wanted her gone. He slapped the side of her head. "Your snot is dripping down your disgusting face. Go get cleaned up."

Eyes red, with one that would likely turn black and blue soon, she shook her raggedy blonde hair and shuffled off to the bathroom.

After she shut the door and he heard the water kick on, he tossed an extra hundred on the bed and took off.

Heading back to work, he considered his plans for the rest of the day. He'd hit the gym and shower before heading home. Couldn't have his wife smelling the skank currently coating his skin.

He rolled his shoulders and steered his Audi onto the freeway. His employer had offered to hire him a driver, but then his boss, Lennox Demetri would know his whereabouts and far too much about his personal business. He was already under enough scrutiny from that cagey bitch, Deloris. Luckily, Demetri's head of security hadn't discovered his major faux pas with Infidelity a few years ago, but that was only because Karen Flores cared more about the company's reputation than anything else, even one of her so-called "employees."

After Kellogg pulled into his parking spot, he squirted his hands with the tiny bottle of green hand sanitizer. After they'd dried, he yanked down his visor's mirror and finger-combed his hair. "You are the king. You own this shit. You're VP of Business Acquisition and Development. Spend money on whatever you want. Fuck what everyone else thinks."

He shoved open the car door and headed up to his office. Demetri's father was due in town soon, not that the old son of a bitch would let his son know. He'd given up trying to figure out the intricacies of that father-son relationship years ago.

Kellogg would finalize his pitch on a possible new acquisition then head to the gym. Stepping into the elevator, he hit the button and called his college pal, Aiden. They were due for racquetball tomorrow. He frowned when the call went to voicemail. "Hey, buddy, shooting you a quick reminder we're on court six tomorrow. See you then."

Aiden worked at Infidelity because Kellogg had suggested Karen hire him to photograph new "employees," and because he wanted to know if that bitch or her troublemaker assistant ever broke their contract. He also paid people on the thirty-seventh floor to keep him up-to-date on who came and went in that secret elevator.

Infidelity was an investment, like so many others currently under the Demetri Enterprises umbrella. If anyone ever found out, he'd simply explain he was protecting the company's best interests. So far, Karen and Imina had kept their mouths shut about his failed attempt at becoming an Infidelity client.

Good thing, because if he ever heard so much as a peep, he'd shut them both down...permanently.

CHAPTER THREE

Locked in the elevator and in Imina's embrace, Aiden delved into her mouth, tangling his tongue with hers and tilting his head to get better leverage.

Mind blown, he wasn't functioning on all cylinders. The minute she'd dropped to her knees and breathed him in, he'd worried he'd embarrass himself. Imina on her knees was a fantasy he'd never thought he'd see in the daylight, let alone in an elevator.

But he'd take it—and her. No backing off now. Not after that amazing—and enthusiastic—encounter. They may not last long-term. Hell, they may not last two weeks, but he would get her beneath him one way or another.

Ending the kiss, he eased back. "I always knew you'd be wicked." He nudged her bra cup away from her breast and rubbed his thumb across her peaked nipple. "How ready are you right now? Shall we continue?"

"We're going to keep saying that?" She bit her lower lip and dropped her head back on her shoulders.

"It's working so far." He brushed away her hair, placing soft kisses along her neck.

"Yes...it is."

He bent his head and took her dusky nipple into his mouth, swirling his tongue around the tip. Then he kissed his way up her neck to her mouth. Hungry and urgent, he drew her against his body and deepened the kiss.

She wrapped her hands around his cock, stroking until he hardened again.

Hands on her waist, he bunched up her skirt, pulling it past her thighs. Keeping one hand full of the fabric, he reached with the other, nudging her panties aside before sliding two fingers along her wet core.

She wiggled her hips. "Get them off and lift me. Hurry."

"We're not stopping. I don't care if this elevator starts up again. I'm taking this." After dropping a quick kiss on her lips, he tugged off her panties. "Come here. Wrap your legs around me."

Once settled in his arms, she clutched his face in her petite hands. "Kiss me."

Gripping a handful of her hair, he drove deep with his tongue while centering his cock at her core, and then he plunged into her body. "Oh, fuck, yes."

Imina laughed, her head thrown back against the elevator wall. "I want it harder. Take me."

Rolling his hips, he set his rhythm, driving into her again and again, out of control, and likely, out of his mind.

Her shirt was half undone, and her nipple peeked out from above the cup.

Accepting the invitation, he drew it into his mouth before flicking across the tip with his tongue.

Gasping, she bit her bottom lip as her core clenched around him. "Oh, that's it. Right there. I need this. Harder. Fuck me into the wall."

"Ms. Lesedi?" A voice came from the elevator panel.

"No. No." Imina met his gaze with wide eyes. "Don't you dare fucking stop."

"Not even if the building's on fire." He flashed a wicked grin and picked up the pace, rolling his hips at the perfect rhythm. Sweat trickling down his back, he gritted his teeth to keep from coming too soon. He'd waited three years for this moment. *Damn it!* He'd savor every kiss, sigh, and moan.

"Look at me." Imina tightened her grip on his shoulder. "Watch me as I come."

At her husky command, he felt his cock twitch. "I'll watch you. I'll see it all."

Her mouth dropped open, and she panted out short breaths, keeping her deep-chocolate gaze locked on his. "Yes, that's the spot. Don't stop."

"Imina? Mr. Maxfield?" Karen's voice sounded from the panel this time. "Are you two all right in there?"

Imina met his thrusts, working her hips in time with his. "Look at me."

Aiden kept her gaze as she whimpered and broke, her entire body jerking before she shuddered and released a slew of cuss words that would put a sailor to shame.

Feeling her grip his cock, he hissed out a breath as his balls tightened. "So close." *Oh, shit!* "No. Wait!" He screamed at his own body, as well as hers. "Sorry, I gotta pull out." *So stupid!* In his eagerness to claim her, he'd forgotten a condom. He quickly withdrew then pumped his cock, once, twice before release slammed through his body. Hot streams of cum hit the elevator's carpeted floor. Beyond gone, he wouldn't even try to catch it all. After the final drop fell from his flagging cock, he braced a hand against the elevator wall and gulped in deep breaths.

Imina ran her fingers across his bare ass. "Very nice." She laughed before slapping him then hitting the intercom button. "Ms. Flores, my apologies. Both Aiden and I are fine. How much longer?"

"Oh," Karen said. "Good. Wonderful. I'd say you...uh...they need about another half hour. So sorry about all this."

Imina glared at the intercom. "Another half hour? What are they doing?"

"It's all fine. Don't be frightened. We'll get you two out soon."

"What is the problem?"

Karen didn't respond.

Imina glanced his way then punched more buttons on the panel. "Damn it."

Aiden could barely keep his eyes open, and he slumped against the wall. "Leave it be." Whether he was talking about the panel, her worries over Karen, their current situation, he couldn't say. Sex with Imina was everything he'd dreamed it would be, and he couldn't care less about the elevator running again, because then they'd break free of their bubble, and Imina would go back to being untouchable.

Imina paced in front of the panel with half her skirt covering one ass cheek.

The other very fine cheek was still visible. He grinned and barely refrained from reaching out and pinching it. "Karen must have stepped away." Aiden took a deep breath then ran his shoe through the cum on the floor. "Elevator will smell like sex for a while. Maybe I'll buy it and put it in my apartment so we can revisit this moment again."

Imina's plumped lips twisted. "This whole thing is very odd."

"Odd? That's an interesting word choice. Though I can't say I'm surprised." Aiden tugged up his jeans but left the top unbuttoned. "You can't just pop off and leave now that we're done, right? Gotta stay and talk. Oh, my!" He placed both hands on the sides of his face and opened his mouth wide. "Horror of horrors."

"Don't be a smartass." She tugged down her skirt and picked her panties off the floor.

"Come sit with me." He took her hand and pulled her onto the floor.

"It's dirty...and cummy down here, and I don't cuddle." She sniffed.

"No cuddling. Right. Gotcha." He winked. "Fuck, I don't know about you, but I could use a nap. You've slayed me so you need to take home your spoils." He hadn't given up in three years, and he sure as hell wouldn't stop now. Not after he'd experienced the feel of her, and watched her explode in his arms. He'd always known they'd burn together, but fuck if he wasn't a bit scorched.

"I told you." Imina held up a hand then adjusted her shirt. "Just this moment. That's all."

"I disagree." He nudged her hands from her shirt and helped her do up the buttons. "I know...*have* known for a very long time that this moment would happen, and now that it has, it'll happen again."

She dropped her head in her open palms and buried her face in her hands. "You drive me absolutely insane, Maxfield."

"No, I make you feel." Easing away her fingers, he clasped her hand in his and kissed her knuckles. "Why do you fight against this? We've always had a spark. I feel it every time I'm here. I know you do, as well. Will you please tell me why you always say no, when you obviously"—he waved a hand around the elevator—"want to say yes?"

"I can't."

Sad brown eyes met his. "You said your reticence has something to do with the company I keep."

"I shouldn't have said that." She dropped her gaze and ran her fingers over her mouth. "I didn't mean anything by it...just another way to get you to back off."

"You're lying. Why?"

"Can't we just enjoy the post-sex glow? Maybe see how many more times we can make each other feel real nice before we're rescued?"

"No." Well, yes, he wanted to feel nice, sure, but even more, he wanted answers. "Why, Imina? Tell me."

"I said I can't, and that's more than I should've said. I'm sorry." She crossed her arms over her chest. "Sometimes it's better when you don't know."

"Don't know what?"

"Oh, for fuck's sake!" Imina shot to her feet and paced in the elevator. "We've become friends of a sort, right? And now we've had sex. Let's leave it at that. I won't do this again. So stop it! I can't get close to you."

Passion and fire. Those emotions wouldn't come from a woman who wasn't interested. He had to believe that. "Can't isn't the same thing as not wanting to." He bent his leg and rested his wrist on his knee.

"Bingo." She jabbed a finger in his face. "Yeah, so, you broke me temporarily. I'll admit to that, because, to be honest, I do like you. I *do* look forward to seeing you. But promises and secrets exist within Infidelity, and if I'm ever going to love someone, I'd have to spill certain parts of my past. And I can't."

His mysterious Imina. He'd admit that was part of her allure. But he'd been digging in the past for many years now and had become somewhat of an expert at unearthing truths. "I'll figure it out on my own."

"Yeah." She chuckled and tried prying open the door again. "Good luck with that."

"You know, when I put people in the lens, I see so much. Things they don't want me to see. Maybe I'll photograph *you*. Maybe then I'll see your secrets."

"This moment is all we've got." Imina braced both hands on her hips and faced him.

"Says you." He crossed his legs, settling in.

"Kind of takes two people to move forward."

"Yes. It does."

Imina dropped down, her knees on either side of his thighs. "Things are better when you're not talking." She cupped his face and kissed him.

Not rushed. Not panicked, just slow, long, and wet. She teased him with her tongue, played with his lips, nipping and licking. As far as distractions went, this worked. Aiden joined her in the play, running his fingers up and down her arms then her thighs, his body heating again.

Gasping, she kissed him harder then reached between his legs, pressing on his reinvigorated cock.

The elevator lights flashed.

He blinked as she pulled away, the haze of lust disappearing far too quickly from her eyes.

The elevator jerked, groaning as it roared to life and began its descent.

Imina sat back on her heels and grinned. "Thanks for a wild time, Maxfield."

Each floor number on the panel lit up as they dropped to the ground level—and reality. Ten, nine, eight...the end of this life-changing moment coming too soon.

He glanced at her but her gaze remained on the lights, the glow reflecting in her brown eyes.

Just before the doors opened, he clasped Imina's hand and pulled her against his body. "You're welcome, Lesedi. I look forward to seeing you again." He smirked, kissed her hard, and then helped her to her feet.

The elevator doors slid open.

Two firemen stood outside. The one with the handlebar mustache said, "Everything okay?"

Aiden squeezed Imina's hand. "Everything's perfect."

CHAPTER FOUR

Aiden grimaced as his tennis shoes squeaked across the racquetball court. He grabbed a towel from inside his gym bag and wiped the sweat from his brow. Kellogg hadn't beaten him. They'd played two matches, and Aiden had hit fifteen points easily during each game. Like always. And, like always, Kellogg cursed and carried on, but the words were all in good fun.

They'd been roommates at Columbia University. Great guy, although he worked a lot. Kellogg had set up Aiden's job at Infidelity. Kellogg was like that, always offering to help a friend. Aiden hadn't needed the job. But, Kellogg didn't understand his financial status, which made sense, his friend couldn't fathom making money from taking pictures.

Imina had been right about one thing, Aiden did come from old money and had inherited at twenty-one. Not that he rested on his laurels. Over the past five years, he'd focused on creating books that chronicled America's history through pictures. His books had won many awards and had been featured in *TIME* magazine. He loved delving into the past, and the East Coast was loaded with stories just waiting for him and his camera to bring them to life.

He glanced at his friend. Mr. All-American, with his dirty blond hair and blue eyes. He'd always been a slick-looking dude. He'd tried to talk Aiden into a salon day once before. He liked the guy, but not enough to get his bits waxed or his nails filed. *Hell no!* The guy had always been fastidious. Designer clothes. Shoes. Hair products. Yet, he'd always been private about his personal life, generally choosing his job as a main topic of conversation.

Aiden took a long swig from his water bottle. "Great game. I needed that." After his experience with Imina yesterday, he'd needed a distraction from thoughts of soft skin and lustful moans.

Now that he thought about it, had Kellogg ever mentioned his initial connection to Infidelity? Hell, Aiden's introduction to the company was three years ago. He couldn't remember.

Kellogg also came from money. They were both privileged, but hard workers. Anytime his pal called with an open court, he rearranged his schedule since they rarely had time to catch up. "How are Sarah and the kids?" Aiden tugged his bag over his shoulder then dug inside for his phone to check the time.

"Everyone's doing great." Kellogg wiped his brow. "Thanks."

"Hey, I've been meaning to ask, what's that scratch on your arm? Did I do that?" Aiden frowned. "Looks pretty red."

"What?" Kellogg narrowed his brow. "Oh, t-that…just a cat. Got pissed and nailed me. Stupid fucking pussy." He chuckled and rubbed his arm before grabbing his racquet's case.

Aiden blinked and scratched his chin. "You have pets?"

"What?" Kellogg finished zipping his racquet into its case. "No. Kids are allergic. Plus, they're disgusting." Tossing his racquet on top of his bag, he wiped both hands on his gym shorts. "The neighbor's cat was in our yard. I took him home." He shrugged. "Wasn't happy."

"I see." Aiden studied the marks on the guy's arm. They weren't narrow and thin, but deep grooves, like from fingernails. A woman's fingernails. Maybe Kellogg and his wife got up to some crazy shenanigans in the bedroom. Who knew?

Kellogg slid on his sweatshirt then smoothed it into place over his flat stomach. "So, you up for a protein drink from that place across the street?"

"Sure."

Aiden checked his texts and followed Kellogg outside, making small talk the whole way.

On the busy street corner, they waited for the crosswalk light. A breeze whipped through his hair, giving him a chill. Fall weather was on the horizon. He'd head up north to photograph the colorful trees. Maybe he could talk Imina into staying at his parents' place. A guy could dream, right? He inwardly chuckled, then a hard nudge against his shoulder had him tensing and gripping his bag tighter. "What the hell, man?"

The rude guy barreled right over to Kellogg and grabbed his arm. "Mr. Brown, we watch and we know. *This* is for Nadia."

Aiden could only stand in shock as the guy hauled off and punched Kellogg twice in the gut.

"Whoa...wait!" Aiden lunged forward, but jolted to a stop when two burly men grabbed his arms and held him against the building behind them. "What the hell?"

"...not enough money for what you do to my girl, you pig. Take money elsewhere." After delivering a final blow to Kellogg's face, the dark-haired man in a crisp gray suit spat then turned and faced Aiden. "You should rethink your friends, cowboy." He nodded at his men then stormed off in the opposite direction to a black sedan parked at the curb.

The men released Aiden and followed.

Aiden watched them drive away. This was the second time in a week someone had suggested he rethink his connections. Sound returned. The rush of cabs driving by. Honking horns. Sirens. And his friend's long, low groan. "What was all that about?" He dropped to one knee at Kellogg's side. "What the hell, man? Do you need an ambulance?"

"No. Those fuckers." Kellogg sneered, his face a cold mask. "They'll pay. He thinks he can come to my side of town and shove me around? Piece of shit. He knew."

"He knew?" Aiden eased back. "Knew what? You know that guy?" He jerked his thumb in the direction of the retreating car.

"What?" Kellogg rubbed his jaw, a deep red print visible on his face. "What are you implying? Of course, I don't know him."

"But you said he knew—"

Kellogg waved him off. "Get me back to the gym. Ronez, the trainer, is also studying sports medicine. He can fix me up."

Replaying the event in his mind, Aiden helped Kellogg to his feet then led him inside the gym. Had Kellogg roughed up a girl? Had she given him those marks on his arm? Were his actions so extreme that the pimps—or whatever they called themselves...handlers—tracked down his friend to exact retribution? Had he misjudged this man before him? Aiden swallowed back the bile at the thought of what his friend could do to a woman.

After Ronez wrapped up Kellogg's ribs and loaded him with painkillers, the trainer left them alone in the private locker room.

"Want to tell me what that was about?"

"None of your business." Kellogg sniffed and rubbed his side.

"Who's Nadia?" Aiden stood before him, legs braced apart.

Kellogg shot off the bench. "Listen, we've been friends for a long time, right? Have you ever known me to do anything wrong? No. I don't know who those guys were or what they wanted. Case of wrong identity. So leave it alone."

"I'm sorry, Kellogg, but I don't believe you." Aiden folded both arms across his chest. "The guy knew your name."

"You're hearing things." He shrugged a shoulder then dropped his gaze.

Hearing things? That was Kellogg's defense? Anytime a person put the blame back on him, Aiden had to wonder. "I'm not *hearing* anything. I *saw*. And you're lying."

"I suggest you leave it." Kellogg poked a finger against Aiden's chest. "You think about where you are right now. Think about your comfy little world. You stay out of my business, and I'll stay out of yours."

"Are you threatening me?" Aiden narrowed his gaze, betrayal and anger rising like mercury to the top of his internal thermometer. Who was this man? A liar? A user of women? His college pal wouldn't be so enraged if the answers to those questions weren't yes and yes. Just what kind of man was Kellogg Brown and, even worse, why hadn't he seen the evil beneath?

"Aiden, everyone knows you're an artist. You hide behind your little lens and extrapolate things. Imagine stories where none exist, and then spew all that shit into magazines and your silly little books. My life isn't up for investigation. So, keep your nose out of it." Stepping into his space, Kellogg shoved his shoulder. "I don't threaten, I deliver, so back off, or I'll forget we were ever friends."

Jaw clenched, Aiden met Kellogg's gaze. "You hired a hooker and beat her? What kind of monster are you? That's sick."

Kellogg's nostrils flared as he took a deep breath. Then, as if a switch had been flipped, he took a step back and brushed a hand down his sweatshirt. "If you breathe one word about what happened today, I will end you."

"That wasn't a denial."

"All right. Fine. One time." Kellogg paced before him in the small room. "I hired a couple of girls for a client who asked for a little entertainment. The guy got rough so I grabbed him, and we left. That *is* all."

The story should have unclenched the sickness in Aiden's gut, but it didn't. Lies rolled too easily and too smoothly from this man's tongue. The attack outside the gym had been personal. Maybe a long time in coming. The whole thing raised far too many questions. "How did you know who to hire?"

"Because I've done it before!" Kellogg practically shouted down the roof.

"For work?"

"Yes." Kellogg heaved a sigh. "Now, leave it."

Like hell he would. He fisted both hands at his sides. "Do you know how they get those girls? Where they come from? It's horrific. It's called trafficking, Kellogg. Why would you be involved in something like that?"

"They're whores," Kellogg scoffed, running a hand through his golden hair. "Who gives a shit?"

"Right." Aiden drew out the word, disgust and revulsion ripping through him. "Find another racquetball partner." Done with this conversation, he grabbed his bag off the floor and turned for the door.

Kellogg gripped his arm. "You'll keep your mouth shut."

Aiden glanced at Kellogg then at his arm. "Let go."

A couple seconds ticked by before Kellogg released him.

Aiden stormed straight out of the locker room door, went outside, walked two blocks, and hailed a cab. "Central Park." He needed fresh air. Trees. Life.

He should've clocked Kellogg. Should've held him down until he told the truth. But what more proof did he need? His friend had hired a hooker and hurt her. Whether Kellogg's story of the other guy was true or not, it didn't matter. Aiden's world had tumbled outside of the square frame he normally lived within. But he couldn't hide behind the lens anymore. Imina had rocked his world, and Kellogg had...wait...Kellogg had referred him to Infidelity. So that would mean he knew Imina and Karen, right? Aiden's stomach churned at the thought. Imina had said she couldn't be with Aiden due to the company he kept. As he stared out the window, he swallowed hard. Did Imina know the kind of man Kellogg really was? And if so, how?

CHAPTER FIVE

After an hour of sitting in the park—watching joggers pass by, women pushing strollers, and a flamboyant dog walker who'd stopped and left his number—Aiden finally shook off the fury over his friend's disgusting behavior. He'd speak to his pal, Tony Antonacci, a beat cop who also worked security at fashion shows. Tony might have an idea of how the whole underground trafficking system worked.

Aiden wouldn't leave things be. If Kellogg was hurting women, then he had to stop him. He'd hire someone to trail Kellogg. Maybe Tony could help with that, too. Or his cop friend could hook him up with a good private eye.

He sighed and leaned against the hard wood bench. Light flickered through the heavy canopy of trees. The leaves were just starting to turn from green to golds and reds. Two benches down, a homeless man stirred and shouted a few nonsensical words. This was New York City. The highest of the high and the lowest of the low, but what happened when someone like Kellogg took advantage of that divide?

Aiden rubbed his eyes. While sitting here stewing, he'd missed an appointment with his publicist. She'd sent him a few texts. Yet, he couldn't talk business, sales, or promotion when his whole view on the world had imploded. Sure, he'd known evil people existed, but he'd never watched a person he'd thought he'd known change right before his eyes.

A cool breeze drifted across his skin. He shivered, still slightly damp in his workout clothes. He'd believed he was a good judge of character, but now wondered what else, and who else, he'd been wrong about. Yet, weren't people like Kellogg sociopaths or psychopaths? He'd never truly understood the difference, only that they could hide who they were. They'd learned to adapt and change as necessary. Kellogg was two very different people. The hard-working family man, and also someone who hired a woman and hurt her enough that she left deep grooves in his arm and forced her handlers to find him outside their exclusive gym. "Unbelievable." He huffed and scrubbed his temples.

Ready to leave, he dropped his phone in his bag then smiled at an older couple passing by, hands locked together. Some good still existed in this world.

Sidetracked by thoughts of asking them to stop and pose, he almost didn't catch his phone ringing. "Dang it. I just put this back in here." He dug around in his bag until he felt his rubber case. After casting a final glance at the couple, he checked the caller ID. Private. Since that could be any of his clients, he pressed the green talk button. "Maxfield."

"Good afternoon." Karen Flores spoke on the other end. "I have a problem. Do you think you can help?"

"Is it Imina?" Aiden shot off the park bench. "Is she okay?" Irrational fear raced down his spine, but his world wasn't quite rational right now.

"Imina. Okay? Well," Karen laughed. "That's debatable. Anyway, I'd like you to come in. We had a rather...interesting day, and I need you to serve as a distraction for a time."

"Distraction for whom?"

"Do you really believe that an elevator in my building would suddenly stop, Mr. Maxfield? You know what I do for a living, right?"

Aiden lifted his phone away from his ear and stared at it. "It was you?" Realizing he was talking at his cell instead of in it, he brought the device back to his ear. "I'm sorry, but why would you do that?" He glanced around the park as if the people around him could give answers. What the hell was happening in his life? Nobody was acting as they should be.

"Get here in an hour." After delivering that directive, she hung up.

Aiden shoved his phone in his shorts pocket.

Karen had halted the elevator.

Aiden smiled then chuckled. *Karen!* He dropped his head back on his shoulders and laughed. Laughed until people stopped to stare, but he didn't care...he had the ultimate matchmaker on his side.

———

AFTER TAKING THEIR NEWEST "EMPLOYEE" down to the lobby and seeing her out the door, Imina went back upstairs and barged into Karen's office. "That girl, Alexandria, was scared to death. How could you do that to her? You promised me. You said you'd always make sure Infidelity employees were safe, and yet, she was shaking."

"She signed the agreement." Sitting behind her desk, Karen swirled the amber liquid in her whiskey glass.

"You can take those agreements and shove them up your ass. She didn't want to go. How can you be so cold?"

"I gave her the card with the emergency number."

"Yeah, right." Imina flipped a hand in the air. "Like a scared woman is going to call. Not when they're desperate and alone and being hurt. When you're beat down, you don't reach out. You shiver in the corner, waiting for the next slap."

"That won't happen again."

Imina waved a hand at the door. "*That* just walked out."

"He won't hurt her." Karen tapped her finger against the rim of her glass, creating a ting-ting sound with her nail. "Demetri has never interfered here. His sudden interest in this woman has to be personal."

"Demetri? As in Lennox Demetri?" Imina glared at Karen as she recalled the rumors surrounding that name. "Isn't he affiliated with the mob?"

"No...at least...no." Karen sniffed then stared out her window.

"Great." Imina braced both hands on her hips and studied her mentor. A woman who had seen her at her worst and turned her into the creature she was today. Was that a good thing? Who really knew? "Someone should watch out for Ms. Collins."

"Demetri has a woman who works for him. Deloris. I've met her once." Karen huffed out a laugh. "Was like looking in the mirror, only scarier. That woman will keep an eye on the whole situation. She won't let anything tarnish the Demetri reputation."

"Alexandria isn't a *situation*, Karen. She's a living, breathing person." Imina paced in front of the desk, restless and angry. Sure nothing good would come of that poor redhead's situation, especially with Demetri involved.

Karen frowned. "Don't question my judgment."

"You're not infallible." Though harsh, Imina had to speak this truth. Together, they hadn't always made the right choices for the employees but rather the right choices for Infidelity.

"You're speaking out of turn."

"Someone around here has to." Imina lifted both brows and met Karen's gaze.

Her boss sighed then sipped from her drink. "Sit down."

"Why?" She was in no mood to be lectured over her outburst.

"I want to hear about you and Aiden in the elevator. Anything... interesting happen?"

"What do you mean?" The word—interesting always held far too many connotations. Imina narrowed her eyes. Why was Karen concerned about events occurring inside the elevator instead of questioning why it'd stopped in the first place? "I'll check to see if security emailed a report." Using that as an excuse, she stepped closer to the door.

"Uh huh...that's what I thought."

Imina snapped around. "Thought about what?"

"You."

"Me?" Imina tapped her nail against the doorframe, because this conversation was not heading in a safe direction. Much like her elevator excursion yesterday.

"I just got off the phone with Aiden. He's taking you out."

Gasping, Imina stormed toward Karen's desk. "What the hell are you talking about?"

"I lied about the cameras being off in the elevator, because I'm tired of you flouncing around here like your shit doesn't stink. Yesterday's footage proved that all I have to do is get you alone with the man and you drop to your knees."

"How dare you!" Imina lifted her hands then closed them into fists. If Karen wasn't her boss, she would jump over this desk and nail her with two shots straight to her big nose.

"You two have been dancing around each other for years. Yawn. Boring." Karen covered her mouth with a hand then gave her lips two soft pats.

Imina wanted to do a lot more than "pat" her boss's treacherous lips.

Karen stood and leaned both hands on her desk, meeting her gaze. "I'm over it. Time for some action, so I took it, and I was right."

This was insane. Karen had cut off the power. *And* watched? "Not only are you manipulative, but apparently, you're a pervert."

"Manipulation is my job description, Imina. You know that. Again, don't question my motives or my skills." Karen's gaze sharpened. "Get out. And I mean *out*. Go with Aiden. It's what I want. So, go."

"It's not what I want. You can't just—"

"I can and I did. I made a mistake with you before, and I learned from it. You haven't. So, I'm forcing *this* lesson upon you. Aiden

Maxfield is your perfect match." Karen jabbed a finger in her direction. "Don't fuck it up."

Imina glared at Karen then lifted both middle fingers before she stomped to the door and flung it open. When the door had the nerve to bounce back, she slammed it shut.

CHAPTER SIX

Imina fumed, mumbling choice words about overbearing bosses under her breath. Whipping on her black leather jacket, she trudged toward the elevator, feeling the weight of the day settling on her shoulders. She'd go home. Drink a bottle of wine. But she would *not* blindly follow Karen's plan. She'd done so before and gotten burned. Bad. Yet...Aiden *was* different. And Karen *was* right. After spending that single hour in the elevator, she wanted nothing more than to get her hands on the man for real. To take her time. To make him beg.

Imina took the elevator down, frowning at the panel as if it were the cause of her troubles and not her meddlesome boss. "Stupid elevators." Once in the lobby, she clipped past all the people hustling by, staring at their phones or conversing with the person beside them. Busy, busy. Every time she walked to her apartment, to the gym, or to work, she weaved through a plethora of people. She couldn't imagine a town where she had to sit in long lines of traffic every day, fighting to get to work and back home again. Sure, on bad weather days, she took a cab, but today she breathed in the scents of New York City. Car exhaust, Indian food from the place across the street, and the general mixture of humanity passing by her office building. She loved this city.

Releasing a slow breath, she turned on her heel and saw him. Aiden Maxfield in jeans and a button-down shirt was one thing, but seeing him in a nice pair of black slacks and a crisp white shirt with a gold tie was something else. He still had his ever-present messenger bag at his side, likely with a few cameras tucked away.

When he saw her, he grinned. The expression lit up his face, crinkling the corners of his eyes and revealing bright white teeth.

Before she could stop herself, she smiled in return. "Look at you, all dressed up."

Stopping at her side, he jerked his head toward her building. "I was hoping to take another elevator ride."

Imina rolled her eyes. "Boo, just boo."

He chuckled. "I'm here on orders from your boss. I'm to take you to dinner."

Should she go? Imina tugged on the zipper of her jacket. They'd had a hellish day. Karen had breached normal protocol with the Collins woman. The whole thing gave her an uneasy feeling. She'd hoped to drink her wine bottle alone—her whole bottle, but maybe venting to Aiden would be nice. The decision shouldn't be this easy. She shouldn't want to spend time with this annoying man. They'd end up in bed again. No question. But...honestly, stress relief delivered by Aiden Maxfield didn't seem like such a bad thing right now.

"You know I like to be disagreeable. Karen told me she'd called you. I should tell you both to kiss my ass and go home alone." Turning on her heel, Imina started toward the crosswalk. "But, all right, tonight, I'll go. However, I need wine after today. Lots of wine. And red wine." She glanced over her shoulder. "I want something thick and rich."

He smirked and opened his mouth.

"Don't!" She stuck a finger in his face. "Don't say it."

He tucked in his lips. "Sorry, I can't let that one pass."

"Fine, get it over with, Mr. Innuendo-King."

"I have something thick and rich at my place." He ran a finger across her lips. "Something exquisite and bold. A taste you'll come to crave, baby."

She narrowed her eyes.

He chuckled then dropped his hand to his side. "But seriously, how about I cook for you?"

She sniffed then glanced toward the traffic light. The green walking man lit up so she hustled to cross the street. "You cook?"

"Yes, but we need to stop off at the market." Aiden followed.

His long legs easily caught up to her side. Muscled legs that had held her in place as he'd rocked into her body. Legs she'd love to have around her, above her, and beneath her. She sniffed and pulled at her collar. *Stop thinking naughty thoughts!*

Seeking distraction, Imina stopped on the sidewalk and tossed a few coins into a homeless man's coffee cup.

"Don't move." Aiden pressed a hand against her shoulder.

Heart thrumming, Imina's eyes widened. "Why? What's wrong?"

He pulled a camera from his bag. "Girl in New York."

"What?" She glanced around. "Me?"

"Yeah. I can see it." He lifted the camera to his eye. "A girl making her way through the city. What does the world look like through her eyes?"

"Right now, it looks a little sad." Imina glanced down at the homeless man, covered in dirt and wearing a stained red bandana around his neck. "I bought him that coat last winter. It used to be light blue." Now it was thick with dirt, and his shoes had separated from the sole so much that his sock peeked out. His big toe winked hello from a hole. "Isn't that right, Teddy?"

The man grinned up at her with blackened teeth. The front two were chipped.

Aiden snapped picture after picture. "That face. Perfect. Sympathy, tinged with a bit of that Imina fire. I love it."

"The fire is from that hole in his sock. I'll have to stop off somewhere and pick him up a new pair. What size do you think he is?"

Imina braced one hand on her hip and glared at Aiden when he just kept taking more shots. "You know what? Give me that thing." She reached for his camera.

"What? No." He shuffled out of reach.

"Yes, you hide behind that lens. Let me see through it."

"Is that what you want?" He arched a brow, expression serious, for once.

She bit her lip, because she understood the weight of his question. Knew he meant more, but she didn't have any answers. Not yet. "Yeah, maybe it's time I see life a bit differently. Show me how it works."

Aiden tilted his head and studied her a moment before handing her the camera. "This'll be fun. I promise."

Imina shook her head. "We'll see." She shrugged, but the idea actually did appeal. Maybe, if she held the viewfinder up to her eye, she'd see life within a new frame of reference. One that revealed a picture of hope, and maybe, just maybe...love.

IMINA LEANED BACK on Aiden's couch, sleepy after all the rich Indian food. She needed more wine but was too comfortable to get up. His brownstone was in an actual neighborhood. Pricey, but nice, and a bit homey. The decor was done in warm golds and deep browns. Likely professionally decorated. Yet, just like her place, his apartment was neat and tidy, barely lived in. With so much to do in this city, who stayed home? Not her, and obviously not Aiden.

While shopping for groceries and on their way back to his apartment, she'd laughed as he'd struck all kinds of poses. Happy. Sad. Annoyed. She'd snapped the angle of his chin, the sparkle of gold in his brown eyes, the slight lines appearing beside them as he smiled. She'd caught the real Aiden. Saw him in a different way. He made her laugh, something she rarely did, which was kind of sad, actually.

Sighing, she straightened then placed her empty wineglass on the faded wood coffee table before she picked up one of his photo books, set beside a couple others by Ansel Adams. She'd already looked through Aiden's books. As a matter of fact, she had them all at her place. The way he pictured the world fascinated her. She'd lived in New York her whole life but didn't know the history like he did. He'd dug up very interesting facts, and she'd truly enjoyed reading them.

"Do you need more wine?" Aiden called from the kitchen.

"Yes, please. Although, I don't know how I can fit another drop in my stomach."

He came in, carrying a bottle of wine and his glass in one hand and his camera in the other then he set everything on the table before topping off her wineglass. "I'm all set now." He waved a hand down his body. "No tie. Much better."

He'd changed into a pair of jeans and a white T-shirt with a black-and-white photo on the front.

"Imina, I didn't want to ruin our dinner, but I'd like to ask you a few questions." He stood in front of the table but, after a moment, began to pace. "As you may know, Kellogg Brown referred me to Infidelity."

Imina straightened. Where was this going? Had Kellogg talked? No way he'd revealed anything. She loathed the man with every fiber of her being, but couldn't tell her story to Aiden, which added an ache to her already thrumming heart.

"I had a disturbing run-in with him." Aiden ran a hand through his thick hair. "I understand you can't talk about Infidelity's clients, but I believe Kellogg is abusive to women. I'm disappointed in myself because I've never seen who he really is before. I can't simply forget what I discovered."

"Wh-what did he do?" Imina gripped the couch cushion. They should have taken Kellogg down. Had him arrested. This was her fault. Hers and Karen's That man was out there hurting more women because they hadn't spoken up.

"He had a story. A cover up, which I'm not so sure was true, but I want to say, if he's a client at Infidelity, I'd get rid of him. Whatever you have to do, remove him from your system."

Imina swallowed hard. "He's not a client."

"Was he ever?"

She didn't answer. She couldn't.

"I see." Aiden nodded. "Do you know him, then?"

Imina's gaze shot to his. He didn't *see* anything. And she couldn't talk about this, even if she wanted to. "Yes, I know Kellogg Brown. Demetri Enterprises is the major investor in Infidelity. Kellogg initiated that." She averted her gaze to the photos on the wall, trying to calm her wildly-beating heart by studying the play of sunlight across the glass frames. Losing herself in the deep reds and burnished golds of fall in upper New York. "Those photos are nice. Did you take them?"

"Don't do that, Imina."

"Do what?" She shifted her gaze back to him and swallowed hard.

"Change the subject." Frowning, he braced both hands on his hips. "I called a friend. He's investigating Kellogg. Following him."

"That's the right thing to do." Imina nodded. "If he's hurting women then someone should stop him. I should...I'll mention this to Karen. Perhaps she can alert his employer. The threat of losing his job might stop someone like him."

"I don't think so." Aiden shook his head then rubbed his hands over his eyes. "I don't know that anyone can stop him. I believe, for some people, the rush of power over someone weaker becomes an addiction or something. I don't know. Maybe I'm letting my imagination run wild." He leaned his forehead against the window, staring out into the neighborhood. "Yet, based on the looks of the guy who attacked him, I'd say Kellogg's ventured pretty deep underground to find his prey."

His prey. Oh, hell. The spicy Indian food did a dirty-dance move with all the wine in her stomach. Regret and self-loathing fought for supremacy in her mind. What had she done? Why had she let

Kellogg escape unscathed? At the time, she'd been nineteen, poor and alone in the world except for Karen. They'd made the wrong choice, and she'd discuss that with Karen tomorrow, but right now, she couldn't do this anymore. Couldn't discuss Kellogg Brown. She didn't want him tainting her time with Aiden. Seeking a change of subject, she flicked a hand at Aiden's shirt. "Was he your inspiration?"

"Who? Adams?" Glancing at his shirt, his brow furrowed then he took a sip from her wineglass. "Yes. All the great photographers. Karsh, Lange, Maisel. I love them all." He tucked in beside her on the wide brown couch. "But *you* are my inspiration tonight."

"Really?" She arched a brow and removed her glass from his hand before taking a drink, grateful she'd distracted him from further discussing that bastard, Kellogg Brown.

"You spent this afternoon taking pictures of me. Now it's my turn."

Whether her immediate agreement was due to the multiple glasses of wine, the atmosphere, or the adrenaline, she didn't know, but she was totally on board. After swallowing another mouthful of the robust red wine, she closed her eyes at the explosion of cherry with a hint of plum on her tongue, but she wanted a different flavor. She wanted Aiden. In the elevator, she'd taken him deep down her throat, but she wanted more. She wanted her tongue in his mouth. Wanted to lick every inch of his body. And she wanted it right now. Flicking a glance his way, she arched a brow. "You want to take pictures?"

"Yes." He lifted his camera from the table.

With a sly grin, she rose to her feet then tugged the zipper on the side of her red leather skirt and let it fall to the floor. "These kinds of pictures?" She lifted her heel onto his table and ran her fingers up the inside of her leg.

The camera click-clicked.

She smiled, unbuttoned her shirt slowly, and then sank onto the plush soft-yellow carpet.

Aiden stood then settled onto the coffee table, snapping pictures the whole time.

Licking her lips, she tugged one bra strap down her shoulder before easing away her white bra cup and revealing her peaked nipple.

"Very good, Imina. Now, run your fingers along your stomach."

Aiden's voice had turned husky and deep, yet soft, as if not to disturb the moment. She glanced from beneath lowered lids and lifted her hips while doing as he'd directed. Her heart thundered, and she moaned a little at the feel of her soft touch across her skin. She knew how to pleasure herself, but tonight she wanted Aiden's hands to bring her bliss. She rubbed two fingers across the front of her lace panties.

"Show me what's beneath, Imina." Aiden dropped to his knees beside her, clicking away.

Her lips parted with a slight gasp as she wiggled free of her panties and tossed them to the side. But she wouldn't go any farther. Not yet. He'd teased her for years. Now it was her turn. She stood before him, running her hands through his hair. Then she turned and released each hook on her bra.

"Fuck, you have an amazing ass. I'm going to bend you over my couch so I can see it while I'm fucking you." Aiden trailed a finger over one cheek.

Fighting a shiver, she twisted and slapped his hand, keeping the other in place over her bra. "Since you can't keep your hands to your-self, stay there on your knees and watch. And click." She strutted around him, and then placed one leg on the table, letting her bra fall to the floor. Using both hands, she plumped her breasts before running her hands up to her neck and through her hair. Sheer need shot straight to her core.

"That's it." Aiden took a few more shots then adjusted his erection in his jeans.

Imina shimmied down to her knees and took the camera from his hand. "I think we're done with this for now. Don't you?"

He nodded then locked a hand around the back of her neck and kissed her hard.

She ran her hand along his thick cock still hidden behind his jeans. "I want this. I want it hard. I want it soft. I want you to fuck me on every available surface, and then I want you to do it all again."

He bit her bottom lip then tugged on it, adding a slight edge to the moment. "Right here."

She'd swat his ass for that bite...but that'd come later. "Yes, right here, right now."

"Might take you more than one trip to get *every* surface." His deep brown eyes searched hers.

She knew what he was asking, what he meant. "Well then, we better get started."

A grin split his face before he pressed her back on the carpet and kissed her. That smile she wouldn't need to catch with the camera, because she'd remember it for the rest of her life.

As the night stretched on, as their bodies entwined and heated words were whispered, as she found pleasure more times than she could count, she knew she'd be back again. Knew that in a life filled with pain and heartache, she'd found something real and true in Aiden's arms. She'd found passion, bliss, and a different vision of her future.

Not that she was ready to capture those moments in metal frames and hang them on the wall. She wasn't that much of a sap. However, she did admit...*would* admit, those images were already bound together in an album deep within her heart. Next thing she knew, she'd be photographing puppies and rainbows. She made a mental note to punch Aiden for that thought before closing her eyes and drifting to sleep with the sound of his steady heartbeat thumping against her ear.

CHAPTER SEVEN

The next morning, Imina knocked on Karen's door. She was sore in so many places, yet absolutely refreshed. Aiden had made her breakfast, loaded her up with coffee then made sure she'd gotten off in the cab. No morning sex, though, which only heightened her anticipation. Tonight. She rolled her eyes at her ridiculous need for the man.

Tonight? Again? Yes and yes. However, his questions about Kellogg worried her. Aiden was too good at making connections. She'd signed legal documents stating she wouldn't tell anyone about her experience with Kellogg. And Aiden ran with Kellogg's crowd. If she told Aiden, she believed he might slip up one day. Somewhere, sometime, he'd make his feelings for Kellogg known. Then Kellogg would blame her. And follow through on all his threats to maim and dismember her. *Lovely.*

And yet, she wanted to tell Aiden. Wanted tell someone, because Kellogg hadn't stopped, and she held herself responsible for what he'd done. If she had to go to jail for breaking her contract, maybe she deserved that. When she received no response at Karen's door, she opened it slightly. "Karen?"

"What?"

Her boss's voice sounded a little raspy. Was she sick? Imina stepped inside.

Karen was slumped over her desk, still wearing the same clothes she'd had on yesterday. Her mascara had run down her cheeks, and her eyes were puffy and red. An empty bottle of scotch and a half-full tumbler sat on her desk. Spent tissues were dotted across the top with a few surrounding her overflowing garbage can.

What in the world? "Karen? Are you all right?"

"Good morning, Imina. I'm sorry. I fell asleep." Karen waved her to a seat. "Sit a minute." She closed her eyes and rested her head back on her leather office chair then sighed. "The inside of my mouth tastes like dog shit."

"Would you like some coffee?" Imina hovered just over the seat then decided to make coffee instead.

Karen had a coffee station by a small conference table set up with four chairs. All black and glass. She preferred the ultra-modern look.

"I wonder why so many people turn to liquids as a way to solve their problems. Wine, coffee, scotch. Nothing helps though, does it? Nothing takes away the pain from our hearts and minds. We have to live with it, and I must say, that really sucks." Karen opened her eyes and met Imina's gaze. "Yesterday was my anniversary."

Imina frowned as she removed the half-full coffee pot from the machine. Her boss never talked like this. Never opened up. Maybe they were stuck in some sort of crazy opposites zone. Made sense, since they were both acting far from their normal selves. "An anniversary of what?" As far as Imina knew, Karen was single.

"He died, you know?" Karen swirled the liquid in her tumbler before swallowing it down.

"Who?" Imina needed to sit for this conversation. Needed more coffee. This was huge.

"My husband. He went to Afghanistan after 9/11 and didn't come back. He died over there...without me by his side." Karen blinked as a single tear ran down her cheek. "Without me."

"I never knew." Imina settled into a chair in front of Karen's desk. "How long were you married?"

"I thought I'd just be a career woman, you know? I'm bisexual, too, so I thought I'd play on both sides, but then I met Andrew and everything stopped. I was satisfied. He made me laugh...and yeah, he sometimes made me cry, but he was just so...hmm...how can I even describe him? He was a mountain of a man. A bit older than me. A colonel with the Marines. A career man. We lived in Washington, D.C. at the time. He was so gregarious. Could talk to anyone at any time. I envied that. Everything I lacked, he had. We were a perfect match. And the sex...let me tell you, the man was hung, and he knew how to use that thing. Jesus." She sniffed. "I miss him every day."

"I'm sorry." Imina tilted the coffee pot in her hand, watching a few coffee grounds swirl and dance within the remaining liquid. Biting her lip, she met Karen's gaze. "Love hurts, right? That's why I'm not interested. No, thank you."

Karen shrugged. "Life is fleeting. Love ends. Begins again. Friends come and go. That's why I do this job. Some may see me as a Madame of a high-priced whorehouse, but that isn't what Infidelity is."

"I know that. I get that. It's companionship."

"Yes. Having someone is nice. Someone you can rely on. And, even if you start with a contract, sometimes the relationship works out. I connect people. I fulfill something for others that I can't find for myself."

"Have you looked?"

"Sure. But there's not another Andrew, not in a million years."

Imina studied her normally reserved boss. Karen deserved a break. The woman never quit, but maybe today she could stop for a moment and relax. Do something fun. Get a massage or pedicure. Imina furrowed her brow. Yeah, like she knew how to ease mental strain. She'd been trying herself for far too long. "Why don't you go home? Schedule's light today. I can handle things here."

"I will go home. Thank you, but I'll be back." Karen stood,

rounded her desk, and then cupped Imina's chin. "How was last night?"

"Exhausting." Imina sighed, and then bit back a grin.

"Enjoy that. Let him in."

"Isn't easy."

"Why not? You're too alone. And Aiden's a good man."

"He is. Deserves better than me." Which was something she'd wanted to speak to Karen about but couldn't. Not now. Not when Karen seemed so broken and sad. She'd work on a way to trap Kellogg on her own. Maybe even discuss a strategy with Aiden without revealing what she knew. Something.

Karen tapped Imina's face with her hand. "Stop thinking that way. Fuck what you deserve and take what you need."

"I like that mantra. Take what you need. Should we get that quote framed and hung behind my desk?"

"Absolutely." Karen straightened, tugging on the bottom of her jacket. "I mean it, Imina. Stick with Aiden. He's worth it."

"Maybe." The maybe wasn't in question of Aiden being worthy, but on doubts about herself. The secrets from her past were burying her. She had to get past all the shame and guilt because women were still being hurt. Kellogg's actions had to stop. "I know you're right about Aiden. I get it."

"That's my girl." Karen headed for the door then glanced over her shoulder. "I'll be back shortly."

Imina remained in the chair, contemplating Karen's words. Not only was this opposites week, but apparently also revelations week. Karen had been married. *Wow!* They rarely discussed their personal lives. Sure, they had cocktails after work at times, but the conversation generally centered on Infidelity.

Imina sighed then meandered over to the coffee pot. What would she do about Aiden? He'd charmed her from the very beginning. For three years, he'd handled her admittedly reserved...okay, somewhat bitchy and yes, back-up-off-me-now behavior. Plus, the man was very well-versed in the sack. That alone had her practically panting for more. So, why not? He was a good match, so she'd let this play out for a while. Regular sex. Hot guy. Dinner companion. "Stop mooning over him already. You've got work to do." She rinsed out the coffee pot then shoved it back in place.

Still...Karen was right, Imina was alone. She'd withdrawn. Shielded herself from everything and everyone, and what kind of life was that? Yet, she had to wonder, was she prepared for a fight against Kellogg Brown? Against Infidelity?

Imina thought of the saying, "Hell hath no fury like a woman scorned." She didn't know who'd originally said the quote, but it was overused, and much better said as, hell hath no fury like a scorned woman who was about to kick some ass.

Yeah, much better.

CHAPTER EIGHT

He'd watched them. Sickened by their disgusting displays while drinking coffee. Holding hands in the park. Kissing in the back of a cab. They were too happy. Too close.

Leaning against a brick building, Kellogg rubbed his temple. For two weeks, a trickle of unease pecked away at his brain, giving him a constant headache. Kellogg didn't have time for this surveillance gig, but he couldn't trust the job to anyone else. Not when his secret had already been revealed to his friend. Why was Aiden sidling up to that whore, Imina, anyway? What had she told him?

Wouldn't matter. He'd end it. Do something. Their little lovefest had to stop. If she hadn't already, Imina would spill her whole stupid story. Women did that. Thought they were in love and, because of that, had to share all the shit in their hearts. Ridiculous, but true.

Kellogg waited a week for their relationship to end, but when another week passed, he realized he couldn't wait any longer. He hadn't tried contacting Aiden since the day they'd fought. No sense putting himself in a position where he'd be questioned again. They were college friends, not colleagues or coworkers. Sure, they ran with the same crowd, but Kellogg could easily avoid Aiden at social functions.

He palmed the cold steel blade in his hand, running his finger along the sharp edge. He'd never killed anyone. Sometimes wondered if he was capable. Tonight, he'd find out.

Imina took a boxing class every Thursday night then walked home. She thought she was some kind of badass with her gloves and shit. But, he knew how to tap someone in the jaw just the right way, and they'd tumble to the ground, sometimes shaking, sometimes completely out.

Waiting across the street, he saw her exit then grinned, pushed off the wall, and followed. His dick was like a hound dog on a scent—perked up and ready to find its prey. His entire body hummed on an edge. He'd never felt this jazzed before. Sure, he enjoyed giving pain, but with the knife in his hand, his excitement rose to an obscene level.

Imina wore a red zip-up sweatshirt and black workout pants. Her head was down as she read her phone and laughed.

Probably some stupid text from Aiden. He'd checked on the asshole. His ex-friend had a job across town at a fashion show. Realizing he'd gotten too close, Kellogg slowed his pace. He'd taken this path twice in the past couple days, searching for the right spot to corner her. Once they passed into a quieter area, he marched up behind her and stuck the knife's tip against her throat. "Don't scream."

"Kellogg?" She halted, lifting her hands. "I'd stop if I were you, I *will* hurt you."

He pressed the point until the tip pierced her skin. Blood—warm and wet, beaded on her neck.

She hissed.

"Drop your phone."

"No."

"Wrong answer." He'd been domineering women the wrong way his whole life. His erection was like steel. Though not in his initial plan, maybe he'd take another piece of Imina. He'd had her before. Many times. But this time, things would get really messy. This time, he wanted to smell copper in the air, wanted to make her scream. This time, he'd leave a forever mark with deep slices across her skin.

He shivered as her blood trickled down the knife and onto his hand. Panting, he arched his hips against her. "I've been watching you, my brown beauty. I know what you've been up to."

Imina stiffened before glancing over her shoulder. "What do you want?"

"Don't you dare use that tone with me." After studying the area, he grabbed a hunk of her hair and forced her between two buildings, ramming her back against the brick wall. "I've made you see red before. How about you see it again?" He shoved the knife into her right side, straight through her sweatshirt and into her ribs.

Screaming, she twisted and pressed a palm against his face, trying to force her fingers into his eyes.

In retaliation, he jabbed the knife deeper, wishing he could see it entering her. "Shut your stupid mouth and listen. That fucker, Aiden, thinks he has everything figured out. But you won't talk, will you? Because if you do"—he lifted the blade to her neck and pierced her skin again—"I will end you. I almost did it before, remember? But this time, I'll finish it. Am I clear?" Heart racing, he pressed his hard cock against her bottom. "Is he taking you?" Tightening his grip in her hair, he wrenched her head to the side. "Does he make you scream like I did? Does he make you beg?"

Imina smiled through gritted teeth. "Poor Kellogg, I hear you're up to your old tricks. I made a mistake before, but I won't this time." She threw back her head and bashed into his jaw.

He blinked against the pain shooting up the side of his face.

With both hands, she grabbed his arm around her neck, jerked down hard, and then bent her body.

"You stupid bitch," he sputtered, twisting his forearm in her tight grip.

"Not stupid." Still bent, she swung back with her free hand and bashed his nuts.

Shards of agony shot through his groin, and he fell forward against her back. "I'll to kill you for that."

"Don't think so." Imina elbowed him in the chest twice then faced him while twisting his arm.

Due to the unnatural bend, he dropped the knife, and then scrambled to pick it up, holding a hand against his aching balls.

While he was slightly bent, she punched him in the back of the head.

Stunned by the blow, he faltered to one knee.

"Stay away from me." With a clear shot, Imina kicked him in the nuts. Twice.

Instant pain seared from his balls to his stomach. He dry-heaved and then crumpled to the ground, clutching his waist, praying for the dull ache to end.

She stomped on his hand then bent to yell in his ear. "You think you can frighten women? You think you can hurt them, and no one will know? Not anymore. Fuck the contract, and fuck you."

Fury and pain rising in equal measure through his body and mind, Kellogg watched her tennis shoes retreat. She wanted to get dirty. Play hard. Bring pain. Well, he knew all about pain. Next time, he'd bring a gun, and she'd pay. She'd bleed and she'd die.

CHAPTER NINE

More than a little concerned, Aiden knocked on Imina's apartment door. They'd been texting, and then she'd just stopped. Right in the middle of their conversation, and she hadn't replied since. He wasn't even sure where she was at the moment, because she hadn't returned his calls, so he'd come here to find answers.

The door swung open.

Imina stood on the other side, a bottle of wine swinging from her hand. Her eyes and nose were red. A big bandage covered one side of her neck, and she had a tight grip on her right side.

Aiden stepped forward, cupping her face in his hand. "What is it? What happened?"

"What I always knew would happen." Imina slurred out her words. Then she shuffled over to the couch. Bandage wrappers were spread across her coffee table, along with two bottles of pain relievers, rubbing alcohol, and an empty bottle of wine. Her hand remained pressed against her ribs as she wobbled over to the couch and slowly sat, leaning to one side.

"Did you get mugged? What happened?" Aiden dropped to his

knees, running a finger across the bandage on her neck. "Who did this?"

"I got away, you know." Imina sniffed, her eyes watery. "I took self-defense lessons. I go all the time. Heck, I could teach the class by now."

Aiden sank back on his heels. "And why do you take self-defense lessons?" He tried not to come across too boldly, but this information was monumental. This was a piece of Imina he'd been missing. Maybe after tonight, he'd have the puzzle completed.

"I was beat down." She averted her gaze, sticking her pinky finger in the wine bottle's opening. "I was broken by the same man who tried to hurt me tonight. By the same man who hurt that girl. And I didn't deserve any of it then, but I do now, you know?"

"No. I don't know. I'm sorry, but I don't understand." Aiden tugged the bottle from her grip. "I was worried to death. Who hurt you?"

Her lips pursed before she smacked them together, and then she patted his cheek. "Your friend. Mr. Kellogg Brown. Oops." Eyes wide, she put a hand against her mouth. "Shhh...I'm not allowed to say that. There're contracts. I signed 'em." Nodding, she pointed a finger against her chest. "I hate him. Really hate him, and I showed him tonight." After grunting out a half-laugh, she met his gaze, eyes blazing. "He knows we're together. Doesn't like it." She waved a single finger in Aiden's face then suddenly straightened and looked side to side. "Hey! Where did my bottle go?"

"Imina, look at me." Aiden was doing his best not to shout at her to make sense. "Are you saying Kellogg Brown hurt you?"

"I said it, didn't I?" She hiccupped. "I never told no one before, but I'm saying it now. He thinks he can just shove a knife in me, and I'll stand there and let him. But no, I'm not a victim. My therapist says that. I don't know if it's true, but tonight I got away from him...so maybe..."

"I'll kill him." Clenching his hands into fists, Aiden shot to his feet. "I'll kill him for hurting you. For hunting you down. What kind of psychopath does that? Who is this guy?"

"What? Wait. What are you doing?" Imina followed him to the door. "No. You can't tell. We have to get him another way. I've thought about it. You and me. We can do it together." She clutched his arm. "Where are you going?"

"I'll destroy him." Aiden hated to imagine what Imina had been through. What she'd endured at the hands of someone he'd believed was a friend. He'd been so wrong, and that fueled his anger even more. "He hurt you. He's hurt others. He needs a little of his own medicine."

"No!" Imina cried. "Don't leave. I already hurt him. I knocked him down and kicked him." She wrapped both hands around her middle and fell to her knees. "He isn't allowed to touch me. No one is."

"Imina." Aiden crouched beside her then gripped her elbow. His strong Imina seemed so broken and unsure. He hated that Kellogg had put her in this state, so he'd stay for now and deal with the bastard later. "Come sit with me. We'll talk this through. I'm still not clear on what happened." He lifted her to her feet.

She winced and grabbed her side.

"Imina?" He jarred to a stop. "What is it?" Not waiting for an answer, he peeled away her sweatshirt and gasped at the size of the bandage on her side. "That motherfucker." Never had he felt such a confluence of emotions. Rage. Pity. Fear. Her bandage was more red than white. "Imina, you're bleeding through. We need to get you to a doctor."

"Yeah, he pricked me. That's what he is… a prick." Imina chuckled, but the sound came across as more of a sob. "Do you know where my wine bottle went?"

"I think you've had enough. Now, how do you know Kellogg?" And where had he left his keys, because they needed to leave.

"I work at Infidelity."

"I know that."

"No." She shook her head. "I meant...I *worked* for them. I was an employee. One of the first. You know how they have a phone number now? A way to call and break a contract? That was me. I'm the reason they have that."

"He was matched with you?"

"Yeah. I thought the way he treated me was normal, you know? Hell, my parents hit me. Why shouldn't some guy who was paying me a lot of money do the same?"

"Oh...Imina." Aiden led her back to the couch. What had this woman suffered? He'd thought he was falling in love with her, but he'd been fooling himself. His heart was already splattered on the ground at her tiny feet, willing to do whatever she needed.

"Karen came to check on me after a pretty rough night, and she pulled me out. Kellogg tried to contest it, but Karen threatened to spill it all. So, we swept his abuse under the rug and implemented a new policy in case anything similar happened again. I'm sure it has, but so far, no one has called." Imina sniffled. "Probably scared to. Like I was."

"All right. Tell me again what happened tonight?"

"I was texting you. Distracted. Kellogg came up behind me and shoved me against a wall. He's scared I'll tell you about what happened between him and me, and apparently, he had a right to be." She brushed at the tears rolling down her cheeks. "I spilled, didn't I?"

"Imina." He shifted forward to wrap her in his arms.

She eased away. "Don't. I hurt."

While certain she meant emotionally, he also knew she had to be in pain physically. Blood had seeped through the bandage on her neck, too. "Imina, we're going to the emergency room."

She gripped his hand. "You'll take me and stay?"

"Of course." He squeezed her hand then leaned over and kissed her cheek. "I tried for three years to get us to this point. I'm not leaving now."

"No." She gasped and pulled back, eyes wide. "After tonight, I can't see you anymore. You know now why I'm not right for you. I let

Kellogg use me, hurt me. That fact will always be between us, and I can't look at you and see the disgust in your eyes."

"That isn't what you'll see." Aiden trailed a finger across her wet cheek.

"Yeah, that." She pointed at his face, almost jabbing him in the eye. "That look of pity is just *so* much better."

"Come on." Aiden tugged on her elbow. "I'll call a cab and take you to the hospital."

"I mean what I said, Aiden. We can't continue." She remained seated. "Kellogg hurt me, and he'll come after you, too. He only cares about his image. He'll protect it at all costs." She squeezed his hand. "We had a few good weeks. Let's leave it at that."

"Imina, let's go." Unwilling to argue with her now, he pulled her to her feet. "We'll discuss *our* plans when you're sober and not in so much pain."

"Telling you the truth hurt worse than anything I'm feeling physically." She frowned and held her side. "Well...mostly." She sighed then huffed out a laugh. "It's the emotional pain that never fades. Revealing the truth about who I really am and what I've done. Major ouch. Think the hospital has drugs that ease heartache? Something to help me forget all my regrets and sorrows?"

"Let's go find out." Aiden led Imina out the door. Her hand was so small and frail in his. He wanted to protect her, yet at the same time he understood she could stand on her own. Still, how could he make her see that they were stronger as a team?

Kellogg's actions sickened him. Aiden would never turn away from Imina based on what that monster had done. He and Imina were not over. None of this was over. Not until Kellogg Brown paid and paid dearly. The man was a menace and, after tonight, clearly unstable and willing to inflict serious harm. Aiden would have to ramp up his efforts to bring down his former friend. Far down. Deep in the gutter down.

At first, he'd thought to deal with Kellogg discreetly, but not after tonight. Not now that Aiden had mentally switched from his standard lens to his macro lens. With the macro, he could see minute details he hadn't caught before.

Aiden had spent his entire life exposing people, revealing truths through pictures, and so he'd do the same to Kellogg. He'd expose the man's secrets to the light, ruining each picture Kellogg had created with his lies and his deceit. No more dark rooms. Only vivid truths.

CHAPTER TEN

At a coffee shop just a block away from Imina's apartment, Aiden weaved through the early morning crowd. He didn't see anyone. Didn't smell the bitter coffee aroma floating through the air. He only had one thing on his mind—revenge.

Last night, the ER doctor had explained Kellogg only pierced the surface of Imina's skin, but two inches deeper and he would've punctured her kidney. After loading her up with painkillers and settling her in bed, Aiden had called Karen and expressed his displeasure over the entire situation. She'd had the audacity to remind him Imina wasn't allowed to discuss Infidelity business. He'd given his opinion of that response in a very colorful manner before hanging up.

Furious and ready to seek justice, regardless of whatever papers Imina had signed, he'd called Tony and asked the cop to meet him here.

Dressed in his city-cop attire, Tony waved him over.

His pal was slouched in a metal chair too small for his burly frame with a to-go cup on the table in front of him. Aiden pulled out the free seat and plopped down. He hadn't slept and hadn't eaten. None of that mattered right now. "Thanks for meeting me today."

"I've got a shift coming on, so give me a brief run down of last night's events."

Aiden nodded, and then gave a brief explanation.

Tony tapped his paper cup against the table. "Is Imina willing to report her attack?"

"She's resting." Aiden frowned then ran a hand down his face. "I'll talk to her when I get back."

"Here's what I've got on Kellogg so far." Tony tossed a yellow envelope on the table. "My photography skills aren't as good as yours, but I got the job done."

"Where were these taken?" Aiden quickly thumbed through the pictures of Kellogg hauling an Asian woman from his car into a building with a flashing red hotel sign.

"Sunset Park. Just off Fifty-Ninth." Tony shook his head. "Your uptown boy's visiting Brooklyn's Chinatown."

Aiden winced. "Did he hurt her?"

"No." Tony crumpled the cup in his beefy hand. "I called a few cops from the area. Informed them they had a live one at this hotel. I stuck around the parking lot until they knocked on the door. They took the girl with them."

"Good." Aiden slid the photos back into the envelope. How many women had Kellogg hurt? How had he gotten away with his behavior for so long? The whole thing disturbed him on so many levels.

"What are your plans for those photos?" Tony ticked his head toward the envelope.

"I'm taking them to someone who can really fuck up Kellogg's world."

"Who?"

He grinned. "His boss, Lennox Demetri."

———

AIDEN HAD MET Lennox before at social events. Seemed like a decent man. He hadn't seen him after his wife had died, because

Lennox had become somewhat of a recluse, likely building his empire. He'd heard the rumors floating about regarding the mafia ties. Through his research, he'd discovered actual truth existed within those rumors. Lennox's father, Oren, had married the sister of a known gangster. Everybody had skeletons in their closet, but the Demetri's didn't ever bring them out to play. Their business was aboveboard, but sometimes, when starting out, a man had to get a little help. Right now, he hoped Demetri was a little dirty—and a lot rough. They'd need it against a monster like Kellogg Brown.

"Mr. Maxfield, Mr. Demetri will see you now."

The leggy blonde with her hair in a bun was the picture-perfect assistant for a man sitting at the top of the business world. Upon entering, Aiden stuttered back a step. He wasn't meeting with the younger Demetri, but senior, Oren. Considering his thoughts on the man's mafia ties, perhaps this was better. Oren Demetri had aged well. Salt-and-pepper hair, broad shoulders, and light blue eyes. A fit man, who looked as if he'd feel just as home on the docks as he did in the boardroom.

After exchanging pleasantries, Oren directed Aiden to get to the heart of his visit.

Aiden appreciated the man's frankness and, once again today, explained the order of events as he knew them. Described the day outside the racquetball courts before handing over the photos he'd received from Tony. He hadn't mentioned Imina yet, as he wanted to keep her secret for as long as possible. "As you can see, Kellogg hasn't stopped."

"These photos do not show him actually hurting the woman." Oren arched a dark brow. "You understand, I must know without a doubt that this man has hurt someone."

"He has." Aiden straightened in his seat. "Last night, he stalked, stabbed, and threatened to rape a woman I care about, and...he *has* hurt her before."

"Her name?" Oren waved a hand before him.

Aiden studied the older man for a moment then shook his head. "I won't give it."

"Mr. Maxfield." Oren cleared his throat. "Kellogg Brown is Vice President of Business Acquisitions and Development here at Demetri Enterprises. His reputation and work ethic are above par. I cannot simply release this man without absolute proof."

Everything Oren said made sense, and his request was fair. Aiden took a deep breath then said, "Imina Lesedi left Central Hospital not two hours ago with a cut against her neck and a knife wound to her side. I'm sure your people can get the records. I didn't want her involved in any of this, so I'll ask that you leave her alone."

Oren nodded and then steepled his fingers beneath his chin. "Aiden Maxfield. I know your parents. Good people. And you, I understand, like history. I've bought both your photo books on New York." Oren smiled and settled back in his large black leather chair. "We're fascinated by the past, aren't we? No matter how hard we try to escape, we inevitably get drawn back. This company, this Infidelity...it's become a bit of a burr in my side recently." He shook his head. "But that's not the point, you were right to bring me this information. Please believe, I'll deal with Brown. I am appalled by the man's behavior. Shocked we've let such a beast work here. Disgusted we've funded his visits with these women." Oren's upper lip curled as he cracked his knuckles. "We never knew. Demetri prides itself on our security, within and without. This breach is inexcusable and will be remedied today." He punched a couple buttons on the desk phone. "Mrs. Rye, ask the head of Human Resources to come to my office in ten minutes, please."

"*Yes, sir.*"

"I will, of course, verify your words." Demetri lifted a hand. "You know the old saying, trust but verify."

"Thank you." Aiden leaned forward, resting his elbows on his knees as he ran a hand through his hair. Grateful to this man. The bricks in Kellogg's life were beginning to tumble. He needed to get back to Imina. He trusted Oren to take care of Brown. Something in the older man's eyes spoke of pain, regret, and a steel will. If ever a person needed a champion, he believed Oren Demetri would fit the bill.

"This woman. Imina. She means something to you, yes?" Oren rounded his desk then stopped and leaned against the front.

"She does." Aiden stood and settled his bag on his shoulder.

"Then be worthy of her. Stay strong and remain at her side. Those are the women who change us. Make us better men. We're nothing without them."

"I agree."

Oren patted his shoulder. "Just remember, don't stay stuck in the past. It's a nice place to visit from time to time, but sometimes it's better to forget."

"That may be the case, Mr. Demetri, but one thing I will never forget is your assistance today. You have my gratitude."

"No issue at all. Once I do a little digging of my own, Mr. Brown will be gone from this building today. I'm sure we'll be fighting his contract, but...well, we have insurance against that, don't we?" Oren tapped the envelope against his palm and met Aiden's gaze.

His blue eyes narrowed, intense like the center of a flame, burning from within. *Whoa.* Aiden was glad he'd chosen photography and not the boardroom, especially if men like Oren Demetri were sitting at the table.

"We'll look into ways to help his wife and children. But, that is all I'll offer him. Anyone who hurts women deserves retribution. And retribution and I are old friends." He clenched the envelope in his hand, crumpling the paper.

Chills ran down Aiden's spine. He had no doubt the man standing beside him would make Kellogg Brown face his reckoning. Not only here, but in a dark alley somewhere. With a bat and brass knuckles. Yet, Aiden couldn't muster any sympathy. Not when he pictured Imina curled up on the emergency room bed, dealing with the pain of two knife wounds.

As he left Oren's office, he smiled. Not all blows were dealt with fists, some were much more powerful and only required a few words. As he pushed past the lobby doors out into sunshine, he considered the next steps, because now that Kellogg was outed, he'd come gunning for Imina. His ego wouldn't allow a woman to best him. Aiden would speak to Tony and shore up security, because Kellogg Brown wasn't ever touching Imina again.

CHAPTER ELEVEN

Kellogg heaved his box of personal items into the tiny trunk of his all-black Audi. "God damn it!" he shouted, and his words echoed through the parking garage.

The two security guards who escorted him from the building remained standing beside the elevator.

"What the fuck are you looking at?" They were morons who couldn't find real jobs. Why were they staring? Laughing? They were fleas. Nothing compared to him. "You're just dropouts who spend more time with weight sets than your dicks."

The blond one grinned and shook his head. "Mr. Demetri gave you fifteen minutes to leave. Time's almost up." He tapped his wrist.

"I'll leave when I'm ready to leave." After flipping off the security guy, Kellogg opened his car door and shoved his key into the ignition. "Mr. *Demetri* can kiss my ass. Comes into my office. Throws photos in my face and tells me I'm out. Who the hell does he think he is? I have a contract." He rolled down his window and yelled at the two security guards. "I have a contract, you fuckers. I'll come back, and when I do, you two shitheads are gone."

"Exit's that way, Mr. Brown." The blond jerk pointed at the word Exit painted in black on the concrete wall.

"That's right, I'm *Mr.* Brown to you." Kellogg revved his engine then whipped through the garage and out onto the street. Horns blared as he exited, but he didn't care.

Someone had talked, and he knew exactly who.

Imina Lesedi.

Somehow, she'd spilled to Oren Demetri. But how much had she told him? Didn't matter. He'd sue her ass. Bury her. No. No. He'd *really* bury her. Six feet under. Dead. He'd already purchased a gun off one of his last tricks. The .45 remained in a plastic bag with prints from whoever else had handled it before.

Growling, he stomped on the brakes at a stoplight. He'd worked hard his whole life. He didn't deserve to be tossed out like a piece of garbage based on some stupid cunt's word. He'd bring in lawyers. Sue Demetri Enterprises. Sue Infidelity. And, at the same time, expose their connection to the press. Everyone would know what kind of companies Demetri Enterprises had under their umbrella. He'd reveal all their secrets.

But right now, he'd go home, fuck his wife, and think. Imina Lesedi had to die. No question. She held too many truths. If she was no longer around to speak them, then things might go a little easier for him. Demetri's investigators would never find any of the other women he'd smacked around. They were nothing. Nobodies. But Imina was different. Imina fought back, and because of that, she had to die. Slowly, covered in blood, suffering, but dead. And Aiden. He'd take care of that worthless piece of shit, too.

Nobody made a fool out of Kellogg Brown. Once he finished her, he'd return to his job, and Oren Demetri would owe him one hell of an apology.

CHAPTER TWELVE

A week after he'd visited Oren Demetri, Aiden sipped his coffee while sitting in a tiny bistro's booth beside Imina. A stubby candle's flame flickered in the center of the wood table. The scent of tomato soup and baked bread lingered in the air. He'd finished another Infidelity photo shoot, so he'd waited around for her to be done for the day so they could have dinner.

After downloading a location app into her phone, he pressed it into her hand. "Thank you. This eases my mind." He smiled before popping another of her croutons into his mouth. The woman never ate them with her salad. She thought putting "stale" bread on vegetables was weird. Crazy girl.

"I got away from Kellogg before." Imina tapped her phone against her palm before setting it on the table. "I appreciate your concern, but as I said before, I don't need all these security measures."

Aiden glanced toward the exit. While he appreciated her belief she could handle herself in another fight, he'd taken precautions. He'd finally spent some of his trust fund on a good cause. A keep-Imina-safe cause. Tony had directed him to a few discreet men who basically followed Imina around at all times, and she was none the wiser. He'd met them both and approved. They'd remain her shadow until Kellogg Brown made his move. And he would.

No way that narcissist would let Imina get away with destroying his life. His loss of employment had been a blip in business news. Oren Demetri had likely done everything he could to keep his company's reputation safe. The press would normally eat up a story this salacious, but the Demetri influence knew no bounds, which actually played in Aiden's favor. The more humiliation heaped on Kellogg Brown, the more likely he'd attack like a chained dog left out in the raw elements for far too long.

Aiden reached over and took Imina's hand. "I believe we've worked out a suitable solution in the security argument. Let's not dredge it back up."

She smiled and kissed his cheek. "We have. Although, I do like to argue."

"No. Really?" He placed a hand upon his chest. "*You* like to argue? I never would have guessed."

"Smart mouth." She rolled her eyes then leaned closer and whispered in his ear, "I can think of better things to do with your mouth."

Completely on board with that idea, he gripped the back of her neck and tilted her head at the perfect angle before kissing her a little too enthusiastically for such a public place. However, they were in a back booth and the lighting was low, so he delved a little deeper, tangling his tongue with hers. He eased back and studied her wet lips then ran his thumb along her jaw. "So beautiful. And so mine." He let his finger trail down her neck and then even farther still to brush against her peaked nipple, hidden beneath a thin red sweater.

She shivered then slid her hand along his inner thigh before working upward and unzipping him. Slipping inside, she wrapped her cool fingers around his raging-hot erection. "I never believed I'd have this. This freedom. These feelings for you. Maybe we had to be friends first. Maybe I had to trust you. But I'm all in. You're mine, too, and I plan on taking you home and showing you what that means."

Aiden's shaft thickened at the thought. His woman was very

creative and enthusiastic in bed. The perfect partner. He wrapped his hand around hers. She'd opened his dress pants enough to brush her thumb across his wet slit. "My naughty girl." He drew her closer for a real kiss. A deep, I'm-going-to-fuck-you-into-the-mattress-kiss. His mouth slanted over hers, again and again. He arched his hips as she tightened her grip on his cock. "Finish it." He kissed his way down her neck. "Right here." He nipped her earlobe.

She squeezed his cock then worked her hand up and down. "This what you want?"

Groaning against her neck, he gritted his teeth. "Yes, please." Pure pleasure shot from his cock and travelled through his body. He looked around the small restaurant. Only two other diners were inside, as this was more of a lunch destination.

One of the two men met his gaze then winked.

Somehow, that made the moment that much hotter. He knew what they were doing.

Aiden tugged on Imina's hair and met her gaze. "Someone's watching."

She laughed. "I hope so." Pulling her hand free from his slacks, she licked her index finger before switching her gaze to the men in the other booth.

The blond grinned and shook his head before whispering to the man at his side.

Imina grinned back then cupped Aiden's chin before kissing him. While sucking on his tongue, she pressed her hand against his crotch, rubbing back and forth.

Sliding his fingers into her hair, he took over the kiss, using slow, long strokes of his tongue. Then, he changed the pace and went from frantic to easy and languid before pressing his hand against hers. "I'm close."

She licked her lips before slipping her hand inside. Her hand worked up and down his cock once more. "Are they still watching?"

Aiden glanced over her shoulder. "Yes."

Her breath hitched. "Then finish. Look at them as you finish." While kissing his neck, she increased her pace with her hand.

Pulse racing, his muscles tight, he bit his lip and met the gaze of the blond.

The man's eyes widened then he smirked before nudging his friend.

"You like that, don't you? People watching," Imina whispered against his ear. "I'm punishing you when we get home. Only *I* should see your pleasure, but you're sharing it, aren't you?"

His balls tightened, and he gasped. "Yes. They're kissing now."

"Are they?" Imina trailed her tongue along his ear. "Then give them a final show. Come for me, Aiden. Let them see."

His hips arched into her hand. One more, he only needed one more hard...

A throat cleared. Then the waiter stood between him and the blond. "I think you two are ready for your check. This is a public place. And your little display is...well...it's not right."

"But...no. We're not done," Aiden choked out.

Imina laughed and kept her hand moving against his flagging dick.

Heart thumping, Aiden swallowed hard and glared at the waiter. "Come back with the check."

He rolled his eyes, and then walked away, mumbling, "I'm in the middle of a very bad porno."

The damn woman had removed her hand and placed it on his thigh. His voyeur friends were gone. A jittery waiter with black pants and a stained white button-down shirt had ruined the whole moment. "Not funny." Aiden groaned. Then, dropping his elbow against the table, he pressed his head against his palm. He rubbed his eyes as a wave of dizziness struck. Not a normal reaction to being cock-blocked. "Imina...I-I'm not feeling so well."

She chuckled. "I imagine."

"No." He blinked again and raised his head to meet her gaze, even though the motion seemed weighted down by a ton of bricks. "Something isn't right."

Imina stiffened, gripping his thigh like a vise.

He shook his head, trying to clear his blurry vision. "Wha iss siiit?" His tongue felt heavy in his mouth. "Whhha?"

Gripping the table, he glanced at Imina, but her gaze was locked on the waiter.

No, not the waiter.

Kellogg.

Was Kellogg Brown the waiter?

What? No. Not the waiter.

Aiden shoved to his feet, but his legs were like two wet noodles. Instead, he shifted forward and jostled the table. His coffee tumbled and poured dark liquid across the table. The salt shaker landed on the floor, spilling white across the tiles.

Imina had to run. Had to run...

"Coffee." He spoke, but the word seemed to come from far away. Someone had drugged his coffee. His food. Something. "Imm..." He tried to scream her name. Tried to reach for her hand, but it was moving away from him, locked in another man's hand. *No. Stop.*

Head spinning, he blinked once more then crumpled to the floor and saw nothing but black.

CHAPTER THIRTEEN

Sink or swim. Those words kept repeating over and over in her mind as Imina followed Kellogg. He had a gun pressed to her side, and he'd already shot a round into a dishwasher's chest back at the restaurant. She'd been kicking and screaming, but once that gun fired, reverberating through her body and ringing through her ears, she'd stopped. He'd lost his fucking mind. He was willing to kill, so she had to get in the same mind-frame and fast.

She had a gun, too. Something Aiden didn't know. She'd taken to wearing her bra holster for her .22. The smaller gun fit snugly at her side, just beneath and to the side of her left breast. She knew how to use it. Would use it.

She blocked all thoughts of Aiden's glassy eyes and wobbly legs as he'd tumbled against the table. He'd be all right. He was safe. Had to be. Better to be blacked out than following a psycho to some secret lair. However, since Kellogg was dragging her though a back alley, he might not reach his secluded spot. Alleys in New York City weren't nice places. Where was a nasty mugger when you needed one?

"...think you can just ruin my life." Kellogg continued his verbal rampage. "My wife left me. My kids hate me. We're finished. And all because you couldn't keep your mouth shut. Well, I'll to shut it for you." Kellogg wrenched her arm farther behind her back.

Maybe she could enrage him enough that he'd act out on the street. She had no idea where he was taking her, but she didn't want to get in a car or be alone in a hotel room with him. She'd been there, done that, and such scenarios weren't on her to-do list. Ever. "You deserve to wallow in shit." Imina screamed the words. "What you did to me...what you did to those girls. You deserve to lose everything. I let you manipulate me into signing that contract. Big mistake. I won't make it again. Everyone! Everyone will know that Kellogg Brown can only get it up if he's beating a woman!"

He couldn't gag her. Not without causing even more of a scene. As it was, a few New Yorkers glanced their way and arched their brows. They were out of the alley now and walking down a street lined with cars.

Yanking on her arm, he bent his head and spoke in her ear. "They don't care. They've got their faces in their phones. Say whatever you want, bitch. Soon, your mouth will be too full to speak."

Imina gritted her teeth. "Full? From you? Not with that pencil dick."

He slammed her against a black car on the side of the street. "Shut your filthy mouth."

"Make me." She glared.

He grinned. "I won't. I won't. No. No. No. Not here. I'll wait." Sweat poured down the side of his face. "I'm taking you back. You'll learn the lesson I didn't teach you before. But you won't go slow...oh, no...you need extensive study, and I'll give it to you."

"Stupid." Heart racing, Imina met his wild-eyed gaze. "Taking me back to the same hotel is stupid. It's the first place they'll look. You're not real good at this capture and torture thing."

"Aren't I? We've arrived." After stuffing the gun in waistband, he reached around her to open the door. "Get in the car."

"No." Imina lifted both hands by her face, taking a boxer stance.

"I won't go down this time." He reared back with his fist and fired forward.

She slipped to the side, and his blow landed on her bicep. Bouncing on her feet, she threw a couple jabs.

He grabbed her hand, twisted her arm, and punched her in the ribs twice.

That was the ticket, because she hadn't healed completely after his stabbing. Grunting, she shoved him away. But not far enough...

He delivered one perfect uppercut, striking the right spot on her chin.

Her head rocked back, and stars formed behind her lids. Rubbing her chin, she blinked back the pain tingling down the side of her face. "That's enough!" Eyes narrowed, she charged forward.

He stepped back, pulled out his gun, and shot her in the leg.

Fire seared through her thigh. "You stupid jackass!" Glancing around, she caught sight of people staring and pointing. A few were even taking videos. "Help! He shot me! Call the police."

Kellogg fired wildly into the crowd then shoved her inside the car.

People screamed and scattered.

Blood pooled on her black pant leg, making the fabric darker. Clenching her jaw, she shoved against the car door.

"Stop." Clutching a fistful of her hair, Kellogg wrenched back her head. "Let go of the handle, or I'll fire into the crowd again."

"Go ahead. You're out of bullets." She wasn't one hundred percent sure of this, but he might be stupid enough to believe her.

He aimed the gun at her head. "I've got enough to finish you off right now."

"If you say so." Heart racing, Imina drew in a long breath. She still had her phone. She had her gun. She had resolve.

Sires blared in the distance. Videos were taken. She'd been shot.

Every action she took from here on out was justified.

Sink or swim.

Pressing a hand against her leg, she breathed through the throbbing pain. Down, but not out.

He'd put up a good fight, but she wasn't going down. Not again. Not ever.

CHAPTER FOURTEEN

Aiden rubbed his aching temples while sitting in the passenger seat of Tony's squad car. The pungent spices from the Asian restaurant beside the hotel fired up his nose and added to his throbbing headache.

Tony hung up his phone and heaved a long sigh. "The dishwasher was DOA."

Aiden's stomach sank. "So, Kellogg's officially a murderer now."

"Exactly, which is why you're staying in the car."

He pressed a hand against his heart. "I can't do that. Imina's in danger. She needs me."

"Man, you're soaking wet and still in a daze. I can't worry about you while I'm in there."

"The waiter thought he was helping." Aiden shook his head, and then raked his fingers through his wet hair.

He'd been out. Then, all of a sudden, an icy wave struck his body. The jittery waiter—and apparently also Kellogg's accomplice—had tossed a bucket of icy water onto Aiden's unconscious form. While Aiden had been spitting out water, he'd tried to comprehend the waiter's rambling apology. Apparently, Kellogg had paid the waiter.

The waiter had drugged his coffee. Aiden had passed out. Woke up. Imina was gone. And now, Kellogg was a murderer.

Aiden had only lost fifteen minutes due to whatever drug was in his system. The waiter had balked and not given him the full dose Kellogg requested. Thank God for small favors.

Now, they were outside the Budget Broadway Hotel. Likely not more than a two-star, which was saying a lot for a hotel in Manhattan. After Aiden called Tony and grabbed the security guy, they'd tracked Imina's phone here.

Jay sat in the back seat. He racked his gun. "Can't wait much longer for backup."

"We know she's been shot." Tony opened his squad car door. "Reports came through of a shooting just off State Street, matching his description. There's video, too."

"What?" Aiden glared at Tony. "Where?"

"Listen." Tony gripped his shoulder. "I'll talk to the front desk. Flash the badge and get the room number. Let's go, Jay. Aiden, stay here and wait for backup. We're going in."

Aiden blinked and shook his head, fighting the effects of his drugging. He had to fight the dizziness. To fight the draw to rest his head against the window and close his eyes.

Sirens roared directly behind Tony's car, so Aiden hopped out and waited by the passenger door.

Lights flashing, a black-and-white squad car skidded to a stop.

Aiden waved them his way.

Two cops exited the car and headed in his direction.

One was much beefier than the other, with a gray bush of a mustache and a scarred nose. The other was Hispanic and looked about nineteen. Their nametags read Kenda and Mendoza.

Beefy guy, Kenda, jerked his head toward the building. "What's the status?"

"We believe a woman is being kept hostage inside. The captor has already murdered someone during flight, and he has apparently injured her, as well. Officer Tony Antonacci and my private security man have entered the building."

"Do we know which room they're in?" Kenda tugged up his pants.

"No." Aiden pressed open the doors and entered the lobby.

Two pop-pops sounded from within the hotel.

Aiden gasped, bracing a hand against the wall. His heart pounded and sank at the same time. "He's killed her."

"Stay here." Removing his gun, Kenda nodded to his partner. "On me."

Aiden stumbled then caught himself on the wood-framed chair in the lobby.

Kenda and Mendoza raced up to the counter, shouted a few words to the person behind the desk, and then headed down the hallway.

Two more cops entered the building. One stayed at the front door, while the other ushered nosy guests back into their rooms.

"She's not dead. She's not." He swallowed hard then stood. Each step closer, creating a pressure in his chest. Yet, he had to see. Had to know. Was Imina alive or dead? And how would he live with himself, knowing he hadn't kept her safe?

IMINA STARED down at the body at her feet.

He'd used her as a punching bag for all of three minutes or so, then he'd stepped back to pull down his pants.

She'd known what was next.

Nope. He wouldn't rape her...or anyone else, ever again.

Enough.

Enough to pull the trigger.

Enough for his death to be justified.

She'd yanked out the gun from under her ripped shirt and plugged two holes into Kellogg's chest. His eyes had gone wide before he'd fallen. As if he couldn't believe he'd been bested. As if all the horrors he'd visited upon others were flashing through his eyes. She hoped he burned in hell for what he'd done.

Pounding. In her heart? Her head? Where was all the pounding coming from?

Her entire body ached. And she figured her nose was probably broken. Mouth full of blood, she spat beside Kellogg's corpse.

The unending thumping continued, louder now.

Then the door to the room burst open. She crouched down, pointing her gun at the door.

"Drop it," a man in plainclothes yelled.

Good thing he shouted, because her ears were still ringing. "W-who are you?" Her entire body shook, and every blow and her bullet wound stood up and said, Hi! Adrenaline rush over, time for excruciating pain.

"I'm Aiden's friend." The guy glanced down at Kellogg. "I need you to drop your weapon, Imina. I'm not here to hurt you."

She swallowed hard and dropped her gun on the stained brown carpet. "I killed him. I probably shouldn't admit that without a lawyer, but yeah...so there's that, and if you wouldn't mind, I need an ambulance."

Imina fell forward onto the bed, allowing the tears to flow. Tears of anger. Tears of pain. And tears of triumph. She'd won. Kellogg was gone. And she was safe. Finally safe. The burden of her long-held secret dripped from her soul, and was carried away by the tears pouring down her face.

"Imina."

She heard Aiden's voice, but had he whispered or was she dreaming? Glancing up, she saw him in the door and frowned. His clothes were wet. His hair askew. His eyes piercing and troubled. "Aiden."

Dear God, what would he think of her?

Aiden tried to press past Tony. "Are you all right?"

Aiden's friend blocked him. "Hey buddy, you can't come in here. Come on. Back out."

"Tony, I need to...she needs me." Aiden kept his gaze locked with hers.

"I shot him, Aiden."

"I see that, baby. You're okay. It's over."

"Aiden, stay back. I can't let you in here." Tony barked the command.

"Fuck you, Tony. He almost killed her." Aiden glanced at the body on the floor.

She'd avoided looking that way, but her gaze cut in that direction.

Kellogg lay on the floor, two blossoms of red, blooming through his shirt.

Waves of nausea shot from her stomach, choking her. "I-I'm going to be sick."

Tony knelt beside her, pressing her head down. "We'll get you out of here in a second. Just breathe."

She did as he asked, fixing her gaze on the nasty floor. A small leaf had come in on someone's shoe, so she focused on that instead.

"Damn it, Tony." Aiden roared from the doorway.

Imina glanced around Tony, meeting Aiden's eyes. "I'm all right."

Another cop was holding him back. "It was self-defense. Let her go. She's injured."

Tony faced him. "The EMT's will check her out." Then he turned back to her. "Even though this is very clear cut. I suggest you hire a lawyer to take care of everything. Let someone else handle... things from here." He patted her shoulder. "We'll get a statement from you later."

Imina nodded. "I was justified."

Tony gave simple tilt of his chin. "You were."

She released a long breath. "Can Aiden come in here? Please?"

"No." Tony shook his head. "He shouldn't even be where he is."

A man in a blue uniform knelt down beside Tony. "This our patient?"

Tony glanced his way. "Yeah, take her to Central."

Imina got poked and prodded then loaded onto a rolling stretcher.

Out in the lobby, Aiden finally came to her side. Her heart skipped a beat as she met his gaze.

He stared down at her, keeping pace with the EMT's "After you get out of the hospital, Imina Lesedi, I'm never letting you out of my sight. I love you, my brave, brave woman. I love you."

"I-I don't..." Imina shivered. He loved her? *Her?* Hadn't he seen what she'd done? In cold blood? Because, she'd known what would happen, calculated everything, waited for the prime moment before she'd shot Kellogg. Was that brave? Did she deserve love? She turned away as a tear slid down her cheek. "I'm cold."

"Don't you dare go into shock." Aiden's glanced at the EMT then back at her. "You need to live. We've got more pictures to take. Don't you dare die on me after I just told you I love you."

"Right, yeah. Love." Imina nodded. "I think...I'm passing out now."

Aiden stopped back as the EMT's lifted her into the ambulance.

Blue and red lights flickered against the walls. She watched the colors spin, spin, spin. Nauseous, she closed her eyes and welcomed oblivion.

CHAPTER FIFTEEN

A week had passed and Imina still hurt all over, but she knew the pain was mostly mental. She stared out the window of her apartment. She'd avoided Aiden's calls. Karen's calls. Food. Sleep. Life. And certainly mirrors. Her face looked like a mountainous region on a very colorful map. Greens. Purples. Deep yellow-browns. She'd likely have to schedule plastic surgery for her nose. She also needed physical therapy for her leg. She sighed and pressed her forehead against the chilled window. Gray skies loomed. Rain was forecasted for the day. This she knew because she had the TV blaring 24/7. Anything to occupy her mind.

Nothing made sense. She'd killed a man. Taken a father away from his children. Sure, she'd saved her own life, but at the cost of another? How was that right? Or fair? In the moment, she'd been so sure. Felt so righteous, but now, she just felt...sad.

Her hands hadn't stopped shaking since she'd pulled the trigger. And she was so cold. She kept thinking of the cop who had interrogated her for five hours. Asking the same questions, making her tell her story from the very beginning, revealing everything. Making her feel as if she'd been the one guilty of tracking down Kellogg to kill him. "No. That's not true. He would've killed me. Get over yourself, Imina."

All the evidence pointed to Kellogg's guilt. Drugging Aiden. Kidnapping her. Shooting her. Beating her. Plus, he'd killed the dishwasher in cold blood. What about that poor man? What about his family? The whole thing was a nightmare she kept seeing in the daytime, as well as in her dreams.

She wasn't quite sure what the future held for Infidelity, either. The police were aware of the company now. She'd tried to keep them out of her confession as much as possible, but everything about her and Kellogg was linked through that place.

She liked the lifestyle her job afforded, but was that worth more than her peace of mind? She understood why Infidelity worked, but being an insider, having to keep so many secrets, wasn't how she wanted to live her life anymore. Again, she sighed and limped toward the kitchen. Maybe a cup of decaf would warm her. It hadn't so far, and at this point the bitter brew was actually upsetting her stomach, but she needed something in there to swirl around with all the acid. She'd probably created a couple of ulcers by now.

Karen had visited her in the hospital, patting her shoulder, offering words of comfort, but her eyes were bloodshot and baggy. She'd been working on keeping Infidelity safe by meeting with lawyers.

Imina kept waiting for a cop to appear, read through her rights, and then throw her in a cell. "What the hell is the matter with you?" She picked up a coffee cup and threw it across the room. It hit the living room wall and shattered. "Stop it! You're stronger than this. Quit wallowing in self-pity."

She gripped her right side. Kellogg had gotten in a few rib shots, and they still ached. Having a fit probably wasn't such a good idea. She rubbed her throbbing temples. "So, what now? You basically killed your demon. Time to move on with Aiden. You can do this. He says he loves you. Gets all giddy and shit. Buck the hell up and love him back."

Love was so stupid. The word was stupid. Saying it didn't mean shit, but she felt something stirring in her heart. Something hard and deep, and maybe *that* was love.

After picking up the bigger pieces of the broken cup, she tossed them in the garbage.

Aiden had shown her a new path. Not everyone would hurt her. Not everyone would leave. Maybe he could show her more and lead her along this whole open-hearted trail.

Easing onto her couch, she read through his texts. Some were funny. Some were desperate. But all were tinged with love and a desire for her to "hear" him. She did. Loud and clear.

He'd seen her after she'd pulled the trigger, and he still wanted to be with her. Wanted to stand beside her during the upcoming trial, and whatever else came their way.

"Stupid man." She grinned and read through the messages again. He'd lost his mind, but she couldn't let him go.

She texted back. *Shall we continue?*

Smiling like a goofball, she used her good leg to lever off the couch and off her lazy ass before hitting the shower. She had a long night ahead of her. Once more, Aiden would hear her truths. And while she knew they had a lot to talk about, she really hoped there'd be more showing than telling. Definitely more showing.

CHAPTER SIXTEEN

Aiden shifted his bag on his shoulder and knocked on Imina's door. Finally, he'd returned to this place. Finally, she'd reached out. Though unsure of where they'd go from here, and unsure of what she'd say, he wanted to find out. After reading her playful text, he'd wrapped up his photo shoot and come straight over.

She opened the door wearing fleece pajama pants and a tight white top with a big purple heart across the middle. "Come in, Aiden."

The soft scent of vanilla lingered in the air as he shuffled inside, placing his bag by the coffee table. "I know we have a lot to talk about, but first, I want to show you something." He dug the photo album out of his bag then took her hand and led her to the couch. Resting the book on his lap, he turned and faced her. "Will you look through these with me?"

She nodded. "Of course."

He handed her the album. "Open it."

Inside were pictures of him from the day she'd stolen his camera, pictures of her in the park, pictures of her outside her building, and pictures of the two of them in bed.

He brushed her hair over her shoulder. "These say it all. Look at your smile. The carefree look in your eyes. The love between us. Because it *is* love, Imina. I do love you."

Her lower lip wobbled, and she leaned against his side.

"Don't cry."

"I hate that I've become this stupid waterworks factory. I'm confused and lost. I don't know what to do next. I don't know how I'm supposed to feel. And most of all...I'm more sorry about Kellogg's family than I am about killing him. What kind of person does that make me?"

"Human." Aiden eased her back so he could gaze into her deep brown eyes. "He hurt you. He would've killed you and then himself. Tony called me today and said they found a suicide letter in Kellogg's glove box." He hated to mention the news, but he thought the words might soothe her conscience a little.

"I know. I saw it on the local new channel earlier." She bit her bottom lip, eyes still watery from her tears. She sniffed. "He had two kids."

"Yes." Aiden hated to see her so torn. She would work past this, he knew, but seeing her so distraught hurt his heart. "Kellogg was a monster."

"True, but that doesn't make it okay for me to be his judge and jury."

"Yes, actually, it does." Aiden tipped her chin with his index finger. "You did what you had to do." Aiden tried to keep his tone soft, but when thinking about that day, he struggled. "I almost lost you." He rubbed a hand against his heart. "All I would've had left were these pictures, and a whole lot of regret because I never told you what you're saying to me in these photos. I never said how I felt behind the lens. What these reveal. Every picture of us shows...love." He brought her hand to his lips and kissed it. "I love you, Imina Lesedi. Now, you need to say the words back. Erase all the darkness inside with light. I promise you'll feel better." He grinned and waggled his brows.

She shook her head. "I took someone's life. Someone's love. How can I deserve love for myself?"

"You can. Stop blaming yourself for everything. It's okay to feel happiness. It's okay to feel confused and lost and everything else you're feeling right now. But feel it with *me*. Be with *me*."

"I am with you."

"Then say it."

Straightening, she took a deep breath and met his gaze. "I love you."

He smiled as all the tumblers aligned in his heart and the organ began pumping began, free and clear. "There. Don't you feel better now?"

"No, but I think I will if you come with me." Standing, she tugged on his hand and led him to the bedroom. "Get undressed, then get on the bed."

Hands on her hips, she spoke in a tone that brooked no argument. Fine. She needed to feel in control. He could do this. Even though, he wasn't sure this was the smartest decision, considering her injuries. "Imina, perhaps we should wait to celebrate. You're injured."

She narrowed her eyes. "Did you or did you not just say, *be* with me?"

"I did, but—"

"Nat! No." She held up a hand. "Shut up and take off your clothes."

After kicking off his shoes, he tugged his shirt over his head, unbuttoned and unzipped his pants, and then he did a little shake so they'd tumble to the floor. "This enough?"

"Quiet!" Frowning, she flicked a hand at his crotch. "Take those off. I said get undressed and that means everything. I suggest you listen." Done with her orders, she turned and pulled two long lengths of black silk from her side table's drawer. "Get on the bed, and raise your arms above your head."

"Shouldn't we have a safe word?"

"It's yellow."

"Very original." He smirked.

She slapped his ass and shoved him onto the bed. Then she straddled him while wrapping the cool fabric around his wrists, tying them to her steel-framed headboard. "If you can't behave, you'll have your legs bound, too. So be still." Climbing off him, she stood on the side of the bed and undressed. "Now that I've got you where I want you, I need to work off all this...emotion...angst...maybe a little pain. I'm going to play. Use you a little, but you'll thank me when it's over."

His cock jerked at her words, leaking pre-cum from the tip. Too much time had passed since they were together. He needed the connection, and so did she. They'd merge their bodies and heal all the leftover worries and distress from the previous days. He'd please her until she understood she was safe. This woman owned him. A fact she was about to make quite clear.

His whole body thrummed in anticipation as she opened the side drawer again and pulled out an index-finger sized vibrator and a bottle of lube.

"Bend your legs." She slapped his thigh. "I want to watch this time."

Oh, hell. Memories of the day in the bistro shot through his mind. The good memories. The sex-in-public memories.

"Aiden likes to watch. Likes to hide behind his camera and see the world. Well...it's my turn now." Licking her lips, she eased onto the bed and sat on her knees between his legs. "I think I'll have the camera next time. Take a few pictures. I like the view." She pressed the vibrator against his dick and smiled as he groaned.

She flicked on the power then brushed the undulating stick across his balls and down his scrotum. "I was young when I first met Karen. She was entranced by my beauty. I was different. Exotic." Releasing a soft laugh, Imina teased his ass with the vibrator's tip, prodding at his puckered opening. "Exotic women should like exotic things, she said. I know someone who can teach you. A woman should know how to please a man. Pleasure and beauty will take you far. And so, she introduced me to a woman. And that woman taught me many things. Would you like me to show you what I learned?"

Lost in the soft cadence of her tone, he didn't realize she expected a reply.

She flicked his balls with her forefinger. "Answer me."

The pleasure-pain of the light tap made this moment even hotter. Hell, yes, he wanted to know everything. "Yes, I'd love you to show me what you learned. Did you practice on her, or did she bring you pupils?" The idea of Imina pleasuring another student, hardened him even more, because she was right, he was a bit of an exhibitionist. But only in his mind. He'd never, ever share her.

"You don't ask the questions here, I do." She turned off the vibrator and eased back. "Are we clear?"

"Yes." He licked his lips. "So fucking clear."

"Oh, someone has a dirty mouth. Be careful, or I'll wash it out." Grabbing the lube from her side, she held the vibrator over his cock, placed it on his stomach, and then dripped the cool gel all over both. "You know where this is going. You've been inside my head for far too long, that's why I keep diving inside you. Now you'll see how I feel." She slid the vibrator along his hole then pressed it inside. "It hurts at first, all that prodding and digging, but then the ache eases, doesn't it? Actually begins to feel good, and then you want it. Crave it." She flicked the switch On again.

"Imina. Touch me." The subtle vibration sent sensations straight to his balls. He strained against his bindings when she pinged his prostate. "I'll shoot all over."

"Quiet!" Leaving his ass occupied, she kissed her way up his chest to his mouth.

There. Right there. Her body pressing against his. Her tongue fighting for supremacy in his mouth. On the verge of explosion, he rocked his hips against her.

"No. Not yet." She pulled back. "I'm not done with you." Rising up on her knees, she pinched her nipples then kneaded her breasts with her palms. "I wish my hands were your hands. But I'm not done showing you. You asked if I had pupils, or if my teacher was my part-ner." She grinned then bent so her breasts swung against his face. He drew her peaked nipple into his mouth and sucked hard. Friction, he needed friction. Needed inside her wet heat. His ass was on fire, sending sensations straight to his cock. He'd played with his sex part-ners before, but Imina was right, she was different. She had enthu-siasm and wasn't the least bit shy about giving him pleasure.

"I started with her. Learned my own body at her direction, then we moved on to pleasing a man. To all the erogenous zones. I'll hit each one with you, but not now. Now, I'm too needy. Now, I want to take."

Thoughts of her with another woman flashed through his head, and he dug his heels against the mattress. "That's so fucking hot. I can see you with her. Envision her touching you."

"Mmm...I don't want to ruin your fantasy by describing her." She laughed. "She was a teacher, Aiden. The students are what mattered. The things I did to them. The things she taught me. Put those thoughts in your fantasies." After giving him a final hard kiss, she rose above him and worked her small hand up and down his rock-solid erection. Lifting up, she settled him at her core, teasing him with her slick center. Placing her hand on his chest, she shimmied onto his cock. "I'm on the pill so we're good."

He closed his eyes. Too many stimulants fired through his body. Her words. The vibrator in his ass. And the woman now riding his dick.

She pinched his nipple. "Pain and pleasure. That combination is all about finding that edge and discovering how far I can take you past it." She reached behind her and pressed against the vibrator.

The tip pinged his inner gland. He felt almost feral—out of control and overcome by sensations. "Take me, Imina. Show me."

"Shut up." She twisted his other nipple.

The pain seared down his spine straight to his ass, causing his hips to buck against hers. He opened his eyes and met her gaze. "Harder. Slam against me. I need it, and so do you."

"I know what you need." Her rolling hips came to a stop, and she bent until her lips hovered above his. "You're not calling the shots here. I am." She lifted off his cock, and then settled between his legs again.

He swallowed hard and sent a message to whoever was listening that she'd do something soon. Hard or soft, he didn't care. He needed to come.

She gripped his dick in her hand then worked the vibrator in and out of his ass. "This the way you like it? Me fucking your cock with my hand while you feel all that pleasure in your ass?"

"I'll take your ass one day," he grunted out.

"Oh, I hope so." Her wrist worked faster over the head of his cock then she leaned down and licked the tip with her tongue. Just the tip.

And that vision sent him to heaven. Two more strikes against his prostate and he lost it. Stars sparked behind his closed lids, and incoherent cries tore from his lips. Jets of cum shot from his cock, his entire body jerked with each pulse, and the whole time she kept up the squeeze against the length of his dick and the press of the vibrator in his ass. At the final twitch, he groaned. Damn, she must've been a very good student. He'd be giving her an A+ for that performance, as well as showing her a few skills of his own. Coming out of his haze of pleasure, he felt her tongue against his stomach.

"Mmm....you taste so good."

Ah, hell, if that didn't have his cock twitching again, ready for round two. "Untie me."

She slipped the vibrator free. It hummed in the quiet for a moment before she turned it off. "I'm not done with you."

"Untie me." She hadn't found her pleasure yet, and that would never do. "I'm fucking you now, Imina. Taking you hard, because I almost lost you, and I need you to explode underneath me. I need to be inside you. So, untie me now."

She crawled up his body, stopping to kiss him, teasing him with her tongue.

"You're just making it worse for yourself."

"I hope so." She untied each knot, dropping the silky strings to the side of the bed.

Once freed, he shot up and laid her back on the bed. Kissing her until they both could barely breathe, he eased back and kissed down her chest, stopping to lick and suck her rigid nipples before travelling down to her clit. "Let me be the student this time, Imina. Tell me exactly what you need. Take it and let me give it."

"Lots of talk, Maxfield. Get to work."

"My pleasure." After kissing her inner thigh, he sucked her pink bud into his mouth then pressed his tongue across her folds.

She arched against him. "Oh, fuck yes. Grade A. Top student."

He slid two fingers inside her wet heat then pressed against her clit with the flat of his tongue, working her hard.

She tightened her grip in his hair then screamed as her core squeezed around his fingers. Her hips lifted off the bed with the force of her orgasm. Small cries poured from her mouth as her entire body jerked.

"This lesson isn't over." His cock once more thick, he rubbed his tip against her sensitive folds. Braced above her, he kissed her before entering her body in one smooth thrust.

She lifted her hips in time with each plunge, biting her bottom lip.

"You needed a hard fucking, didn't you?"

"Ah, yes. Please."

"Needed to forget everything but the pleasure...the love." He slammed into her yielding heat, sweat trickling down his spine and his breaths coming fast.

She uttered a soft cry, and her entire body tensed. "Again...I'm coming again." Her body shuddered, and her mouth opened wide. She met his gaze while crying his name.

Seeing her writhe in pleasure led to his own. Two more deep thrusts had him shouting her name, and his dick erupting in thick pulses. Hips locked against hers, he ground down hard against her body until his cock finally emptied and gave a final twitch.

Falling to his side, he pulled her into his arms before easing from her body. "That's...round...two," he huffed out, while catching his breath. "Round three will begin in approximately ten minutes."

Imina sighed, flopping a hand and her thigh across his body.

The smell of their combined pleasure filled the air. Their breathing slowed to a quiet rhythm. Aiden ran a hand up and down the smooth skin on her arm. He yawned until his jaw practically cracked. He hadn't been sleeping well due to worrying about her. She'd gone silent for a few days. They still had a lot to work through, but they'd come this far. He believed in their future. Believed he'd be right here beside her like this forever.

"I was never a big believer in fidelity."

"I wonder why?" He pinched her bottom.

"I want the picture book. I want that." Imina rose up onto her elbow and met his gaze. "I know every picture won't be all sunshine and rainbows. But we can try, can't we? We can do our best to make the pictures real."

"We can." He nodded and tapped her nose with his index finger.

"You think we'll ever have elevator sex again?"

"I don't know about elevator sex, but right now, bed sex is a hell yeah."

"Ten minutes haven't passed." She pursed her lips.

"You want to wait?"

"No. No more waiting. No more excuses. Just love."

He rolled on top of her, and then bent and softly kissed her. "We can do that." He kissed her all over her face until she erupted into giggles. "That's what I like to see." He smiled before pressing a hard kiss against her lips. "Now, what else do you have in that drawer?"

"Lots of special treats for naughty boys."

He arched a brow. "Is that so?"

"Yes."

"And are you ready to use those naughty treats? With only me... for a long time?"

"I'm regretting calling all my sex toys special treats now." She smirked.

"Imina, answer the question." He folded their hands together beside her head. "I want one moment of seriousness."

"I have no need to answer the question. I thought I showed you. I'm only happy with you. I'll work on the other parts of my life." She bit her bottom lip. "I know I need to deal with all that, but I want to share all my treats with you."

Aiden groaned and pressed his face against her chest.

She wiggled beneath him. "Sorry, I had to say treats. But, all right, serious for a moment...I want more pictures in that book. I want to fill pages and pages and pages."

"We will." He brushed her hair away from her face.

"Hmmm...I think you can be more convincing." She quirked a sly grin. "Shall we continue?"

"I don't know." He grinned back. "Depends on what's in the drawer."

"Let's find out."

And for the next day and night he did, adding memories and pictures to the frame surrounding his heart. A frame that solidified and accounted for all the moments of their life. Good, bad, and every-thing in between captured forever. Unbroken. Unashamed. Unending.

EPILOGUE

Aiden leaned against Imina's desk and tugged on his bowtie. Tonight, he'd be receiving an award for his fifth historical photo book.

But his real reward was walking toward him in a skin-tight black dress that had a single swath of sparkling black beads starting from the top of her shoulder to the bottom of her waist. Her lips were painted a plum color, and her eyes were striking with whatever magic makeup she'd brushed across her lids.

His fingers itched to photograph her, but first, her ensemble wasn't quite complete.

On sky-high black heels, Imina stood before him and stuck an index finger beneath his chin. "Very handsome, Mr. Maxfield."

"You are...beyond words. But then, you always are." Aiden pressed a kiss against her cheek.

Brow narrowed, she pouted. "That's all I get?"

He huffed out a laugh. "I can remember a day when you shooed me away from your desk. My, how the tables have turned, Ms. Lesedi."

She sniffed and pressed her lips together, holding back a grin.

"Well, I do look amazing in this dress, so I suppose I can wait. Although, the longer I wait, the more you suffer."

"I look forward to the fulfillment of your threat." He patted his jacket's inner front pocket. "Let's go. The driver is waiting." Placing a hand at the small of her back, he led her to the elevator.

Imina used her key card then tucked it back into a sparkly black bag.

Once they stepped inside, he backed her into the corner and kissed her. "I'm proud to have you by my side tonight. But, I can't help but feel you don't look your best."

"Is that so?" Frowning, she placed a hand against his chest. "Let me tell you something, I squeezed into this thing and everything beneath, but if that's your stance then you'll see nothing."

"I wouldn't bet on that." He patted her hand before pulling the blue jewelers' box from his pocket. "Let's see if this adds a little shine."

Eyes wide, she glanced at the box then at him then back at the box again. "What's this?"

"Open it and find out."

After taking the box from his hand, she gingerly lifted the lid and gasped, placing a hand over her mouth. "Oh, Aiden, this is too much."

He grinned then pressed the stop button on the elevator.

An alarm buzzed, but he didn't care.

"W-what?" She arched a brow. "What are you doing?"

"I'm stalling."

"Really?" She trailed a finger down his chest then pressed her palm against his erection. "For how long?"

"Not *that* long." Laughing, he shook his head. "Just long enough to get this piece around your neck and appreciate the color against your skin." Taking the box from her hand, he removed the necklace. Three linked strands of pear-shaped diamonds sparkled under the elevator lights. In the center, a square four-carat yellow topaz stone glittered in its grouping of diamonds. "I picked this because it's your birthstone, but also because yellow is the color of hope and happiness, and you represent those things in my life." He fastened it around her neck then ran a finger along the yellow stone. "This jewel's warmth reflects your own."

She pressed her hand against his finger. "It's the most beautiful thing anyone has ever given me." She wrapped her arm around his neck and pulled him in for a kiss then stepped back and leaned against the elevator's brass railing. "You know that commercial...the one that says something about what every kiss begins with, well this one *ends* with a bj."

He laughed again when he really wanted to cry. They didn't have time for another elevator rendezvous, but he'd underestimated the draw of her wearing his gift. The tawny jewel winked and glittered, as if daring him to press kisses all around its square-shape. "Imina, no. We don't really have time, and this elevator...uh, you remember what's on the floor?"

"Yes, I recall." Lifting her lips in a half-smile, she ran her palm along the front of his dress pants. "I'm not so good with thank yous, but thank you. You've made me feel...special. Not something I've ever experienced before."

He gripped her hand then kissed it, gazing into her deep brown eyes. Placing a hand on her shoulder, he drew her close and kissed her, long, deep, and with all the love in his heart. When he couldn't breathe, he finally pulled back. "Shall we continue, Ms. Lesedi?"

"Absolutely. I need to show off my bling." She danced around the stalled elevator, shaking her sexy ass in the tight dress.

Arching a brow, Aiden licked his lips, tasting her cinnamon flavor. Maybe they did have time for elevator sex, after all.

Thank you for reading INSIDER. I hope you enjoyed Imina and Aiden's story. If you did, please leave a review at your purchase site. Reviews are very appreciated by the author.

*Please enjoy the following excerpt from **Ember's Center**, Book #1 in The O-Line Series. Jillian's Contemporary with Suspenseful Elements.*

Owen Killion leaned with one solid arm spread along the top of her flimsy gray cubicle wall.

"I'm sorry," she repeated, then stepped around her chair, almost tripping on the wheel. Her tiny cubicle shrank now that his brawny frame occupied the space. His team's mascot suited him perfectly—Marauder. A vision flashed of Owen single-handedly rowing a Viking vessel across stormy seas to plunder riches from a village. A towering force, he embodied everything she found attractive in a man.

Huge feet in brown boots led to sturdy legs covered in dark-washed denim. His muscular arms bulged under the short sleeves of his hunter green jersey. Shoulders so broad she doubted she could fully wrap her arms around them. His thick brown hair lay neatly trimmed, and his brown eyes were heavy-lidded, yet welcoming, like a sad hound dog. And what was it about certain men's noses that, when combined with the rest of their features, resulted in masculine perfection? The only thing missing was sexy stubble.

He smiled when she finally met his melted-chocolate eyes.

Seemingly aware she'd given him an once-over—a very blatant once-over. *Awkward.* She clasped together her trembling hands. "Was there something you needed?"

"Yes, actually."

His voice matched his body: deep and heavy, and she bit back a sigh.

"I have a small problem you might help me with."

"Absolutely. What is it?" She folded both arms across her chest. *Where are my shoes? Can he see the tea stain on my shirt?*

"I'm glad you agree. You see, I hate when women cry."

What? That was quite the non-sequitur. Laugh lines appeared beside his eyes. Unsure what her answer should be, she replied, "I hate when women cry, too."

Not comfortable around men, especially huge, handsome ones with square jaws sharp enough to cut ice, Ember calmed her breathing and tried stilling her pounding heart. The Marauders' center stood in her cube entry.

Her entry. *Oh no! Where has my mind strayed?*

Did he live up to the rumors? The "O" in Offensive-line raised many a woman's curiosity across social and traditional media platforms since all the players were extraordinarily gorgeous. Not hard to imagine Owen's reputation for bedroom proclivity was very accurate since his shoes were so big, which meant he was big everywhere. *Ridiculous.* She would not stare *there.*

Maintain eye contact. Keep it!

Since she stood at five-eight, she was used to most men being of similar height or a few inches taller—not so with Owen Killion. Her chin actually lifted in order to meet his gaze. Then there was his mouth, which was speaking—

"Ember?"

"I'm sorry. What were you saying?"

"Sometimes talking to a stranger helps. Let's grab a bite to eat." He lifted her jacket off the back of her chair. "We'll go somewhere close by, since we're already downtown."

"What are you talking about?" He wasn't asking her out. Men didn't ask her out. She didn't date, especially not unbelievably gorgeous professional football players. Jocks didn't date chubby wallflowers. Wait, she wasn't that girl anymore. Was she?

"Dinner. I'm talking about dinner." He chuckled and shook his head, evidently amused by her confusion. "We'll walk across the street to that steak place."

"I really, I don't—" She glanced around, unsure how to continue or to determine what alternate universe she had entered.

"Really don't what? You eat. I eat. It's time to check out for the day. Come on." He held open her jacket. "I'd like to hear about your brother."

The gesture was just like the leading man in a movie. But she didn't eat dinner, at least, not a large dinner. Her health plan entailed tapering off for the evening meal, and she didn't stray from her meal plan—ever. "I usually eat soup for dinner."

"I think I can handle that." He glanced down at the jacket he still held in mid-air.

"Did something happen during the commercial shoot?" Some other explanation existed for why he was here. Why he was helping her slip on each jacket sleeve and taking her arm.

"Let's go." He nudged her lower back.

Shivers shot to her toes. Toes currently shoeless. "Sorry, I need to grab my purse and shoes." After hearing his deep sigh, she glanced back and caught him jiggling his keys. "Owen, you play center, right?" As she slipped on her shoes, she turned and faced him.

"Yeah." He raised a brow. "Why?"

With an index finger, she poked his hard chest. "You're bossy."

"You have no idea." He smiled and took her hand, leading her out of the building.

This surreal moment topped her life's unbelievable encounters list. Talking to Owen about her brother would provide another perspective. And that was all this gesture was about—her brother. Elliot hadn't missed a single Marauders game. So she would have a cup of soup in tribute to his football fandom. Staring down from a heavenly cloud, her brother was no doubt blown away a member of his favorite team was in her presence. The vision made her smile, her first heartfelt smile since he died.

And then a familiar ringtone pealed from her phone, and her smile disappeared.

ABOUT THE AUTHOR

She is the co-founder of Healing with Words—a not for profit agency established for healing survivors of abuse, addiction, trafficking, and prostitution. The mission is to bring together readers, authors, and survivors in a positive manner that affects change and relief from negative influences. Writers on The River, an author event in Peoria, Illinois is hosted by Healing With Words.

Her genres are Paranormal and Contemporary with suspenseful elements.

CONNECT WITH JILLIAN JACOBS ONLINE

Website:
www.jillianjacobs.com

Twitter:
https://twitter.com/GreenMooseProd

Facebook:
https://www.facebook.com/pages/Jillian-Jacobs/737689872920933

Amazon Author Page:
http://bit.ly/JillianJacobsAMZAuthorPage

Goodreads:
https://www.goodreads.com/JillianJacobs